I0685828

DRY

Stephon Stewart

FIRST PRINTING, April 2024.
Harry Markos, Director.

Paperback: ISBN 978-1-916968-38-7
eBook: ISBN 978-1-916968-39-4

Book design by: Ian Sharman
Cover illustration by: David Cousens

www.markosia.com

First Edition

For Humanity

The secret of change is to focus all of your energy, not on fighting the old, but on building the new.
Socrates

Look profound into nature, and afterward, you will comprehend everything better.
Albert Einstein

INFERNO

Look after the land and the land will look after you, destroy the land and it will destroy you.
Aboriginal Proverb

A cautionary tale of reality emerged from the universe. In the eternal vastness of the cosmos, the Milky Way Galaxy resembled a masterpiece, as if painted by a heavenly artist. Infinite stars peppered the sky and were uncountable as grains of sand on a beach. The human mind found itself humbled, dwarfed by the sheer magnitude of it all. Each distant star was a testament to the boundless mysteries that resided in the universe's depths. Their ethereal glow portrayed a picture of incomprehensible grandeur, a triumph beyond human reckoning.

In the middle of this cosmic spectacle, a Voice—strong yet burdened by the weight of regrets—resonated through the cosmic void. It rippled across the astronomical emptiness, an echo of unspoken truths and irrevocable losses endured.

"Water was a dream. Water was a God," the voice said, a gentle resonance traversing the incalculable realms of space. It spoke of a time when water had been more than a mere element; it had been the elixir of life, a fountain of vitality. The ultimate symbol of divine creation.

The world they had known had undergone a transformation beyond recognition. Earth loomed in their view, a desolate, ash orb adrift in the cosmic abyss. The vibrant blue that adorned its surface had vanished—replaced by a stark, lifeless brown. A sad tribute to a world robbed of its vigor.

The planet's former magnetosphere, guardian against celestial solar storms, had dwindled to a feeble echo of its former self. It stood as an omen of impending catastrophe, a fractured shield powerless against the deadly cosmic rays.

"No divine creator will save us," the man recited, facing his unfortunate acceptance of their destiny. The atmosphere, a protector of life, now created toxic gases, which encompassed the globe. Pollution clouds saturated the air with poisonous fumes and threatened survival itself. The polar ice caps, symbols of endurance, had dissolved into the chronicles of history. Forgotten forever, without a trace. Causes have effects and effects have causes. "The drought caused humanity's extinction. Not the flood. An inferno," the man continued, his words etched with the bitterness of undeniable truths. They were survivors in a world where life was a daily war, where existence was on the brink of extinction.

In the boundless expanse of the sea, a theater of despair unfolded, a witness to the surreal metamorphosis. From the ocean's abyss, *carbon dioxide*—a captive of ancient depths—levitated with a deadly duty. It escaped into the skies, an understated harbinger of transformation, an announcement that the world was shifting from its own decisions. The atmosphere carried the harsh reality of an overload of ascending water vapor. It was a complicated transition phase with a choreography of elements that triggered an unstoppable sequence of events. Temperatures escalated, initiating a cruel feedback loop: A merciless march towards an unwelcome future. The equilibrium of nature changed dramatically. Heat from the sun was trapped on Earth's surface, held prisoner by the overwhelming abundance of carbon dioxide in the atmosphere.

The sun, a blazing Goliath, scorched the sky with its incandescence, striking the Earth in blinding brilliance. Then, as though destiny conspired for a final reckoning, a formidable coronal mass ejection flare erupted from the sun's fiery heart. It collided with the ocean's surface and unleashed an eruption of energy that shook the core of the planet. Earth's magnetic shield, guardian against cosmic rays, weakened and withered under the siege of greenhouse gases. It was a valiant but pathetic resistance against the forces of a world spiraling towards its own oblivion. Nature reclaimed the water in a perpetual dance of devastation.

The planet, entangled in the clutches of a *runaway greenhouse effect*, carried the wrath of seawater that *boiled* and *churned*. The tenacious assault of the *runaway greenhouse effect* scalded the Earth and boiled away its oceans. Relentless heat enveloped the planet, turning the seas into vaporous mist that mingled with the choking air. The horizon shimmered with ghostly memories of what was once a world embraced by the soothing presence of water, a world that was now reduced to an unforgiving wasteland. Water metamorphosed into towering plumes of steam that spiraled heavenward. The ocean became a crucible of destruction, a symbol of a world unraveled.

Solar winds—charged particles hurled from the sun— swept across the world. This phenomenon was the culprit that caused the oceans to evaporate. The cataclysmic drama that unfolded on Mars eons ago found its eerie footprint on the planet. Earth had transformed into a hybrid of Venus's scorching inferno and Mars's desolate aridity, and no longer resembled the cradle of life.

The world, in the throes of its own undoing, carried the scars of a relentless heat that seared everything it touched. Rivers had surrendered to the sun's undeniable power, leaving behind desolate riverbeds. Proud forests became dead vestiges, their twisted limbs reaching upward in a desperate plea for mercy from a merciless sky. Air itself seemed to shudder in the oppressive heat, carrying with it the fateful loss of a planet that had forsaken the cool embrace of its own shadows. In this new epoch, the Earth moaned its elegy through the scorched winds, a world undone by its own fevered dreams. The land was painted in hues of orange and red under the constant flare of the sun. An eight-year-old *boy* emerged in a sprint across the drylands, a lone figure dressed in a ragged radiation suit. Heat radiated down on his muscular frame. An oxygen mask clung to his face, his only lifeline in the hostile environment.

Behind the clear visor of the mask, his young eyes mirrored the unshakable spirit of a generation thrust into adversity. On the distant horizon, the world ignited into a blinding, colossal burst of light—a solar storm.

The man's voice reflected on the past, "I was born into the apocalypse. Solar flares ripped through our dying atmosphere."

As the Earth suffered under the grip of the solar storm, the boy's eyes remained fixed upon a *well*. Without hesitation, he vaulted over the ancient well's stone rim, vanishing into its depths. Above ground, the world erupted with lethal solar flares that torched the heavens and scorched the ground he had left behind.

In the darkness of the well, the boy's terrified descent was a stark juxtaposition to the tumultuous upheaval unfolding on the surface. Another intense burst of light intruded upon the darkness, erasing all visibility. The boy's descent came to an abrupt halt as he plunged into the warm embrace of water at the well's bottom. The impact sent shockwaves of pain through his body. Alone in the depths of Earth, the boy held onto the only sanctuary he had found during the apocalypse. For as long as humanly possible, the boy fought against the currents, treading water with all his might. Each stroke was a battle for survival, but as his strength diminished, he knew the moment was coming when his body would succumb to drowning. The boy became submerged beneath the water's surface, sinking deeper into its unknown depths.

"Mother Nature was destroyed," the haunting voice uttered, its words a reminder of the world's irreversible transformation.

* * *

Miles upon miles of salt flatlands stretched out like a vast mirror, reflecting the ground back to the sky. A picturesque frontier of the new ancient world, its visual nature dramatically different. The long-ago thriving fields of agriculture were eradicated. Soil was now the badlands. Green vanished from the face of Earth. The terrestrial globe remained unsympathetic to plants or animals. Organisms and animals no longer roamed the planet. Not even a fly could exist.

Across this treacherous terrain, glistening white salt saturated the environment. In the distance, a *farmhouse* stood, an outpost in the post-apocalyptic world.

A sleek, futuristic Tesla silently glided over the arid Earth. Its electric engine emitted a gentle hum, a poignant contrast to the eerie quietness of the area. This electric car was produced to be one of the saviors in the past to avoid an environmental collapse. However, the production of the Tesla was an oxymoron. The actual creation of the Tesla— along with the mining for cobalt, lithium, manganese, nickel, and graphite—depended heavily on fossil fuels.

The electric car was envisioned as a savior of sorts. It represented humanity's desperate attempt to reverse the course of the runaway greenhouse effect. Unfortunately, like so many things in this paradoxical equation, its creation came at a price. The Tesla, a symbol of innovation and clean energy, stood as an example to human creativity. However, its very existence depended on the extraction of essential minerals. The pursuit of these precious resources, vital for the electric car's production, required vast amounts of fossil fuels, unleashing greenhouse gases into an already withering atmosphere. In this cruel twist of fate, the invention that held the promise of redemption also contributed to the world's demise. It was a reminder of the complex web of consequences woven by humanity's

13

actions where each step forward was often accompanied by an equal and opposite step backward, leaving the world in an ever-deepening abyss of paradox.

The moving Tesla stirred a whirlwind of salt particles. The impressive car gained speed with each passing second. A little more... faster... even faster... Rubber scraped on salt. The tires fought against the road's grip with a grinding screech. The Tesla came to a halt, a billowing cloud of salt and dust engulfed the vehicle.

The farmhouse stood in stoic defiance. From the sky the sun cast a harsh light, revealing a glimmer from solar panels on the roof. Each panel was a piece in a mosaic of survival, shining brilliantly. Its exterior displayed the scars of countless years fighting the environmental catastrophe. Every weathered plank told a story of resilience. The white paint provided a cosmic, particle-protective radiant shield, a final stand against the blaze of solar fury. Doors and windows were boarded up, a brittle barricade against a world seeking to suffocate its victims.

In the backyard, a corroded water tank remained an artifact from an era lost to memory. Its oxidized exterior displayed the aftermath of countless heatwaves. Dried remnants of clothes hung from a wire clothesline suspended against the unrelenting waves of oppressive heat. A windmill rose on the drought-infected prairie planes. Rusted, decaying blades locked in a quiet battle with the filthy pollution clouds that clung to them. Beside it, a stone well. The rocky structure was an ancient vestige. A God in this landscape.

Sunlight slithered through the parted drapes, casting shadows across the bedroom. An unending ballet of specks of dust danced haphazardly. This particle that had been around since the beginning of time, now submerged the entire planet. Dust descended leisurely upon every artifact. An oil painting hung on the wall. The painting of Earth resembled the days of old. It unveiled a world that had once pulsed with life, untouched by the drought. Now it reigned with pitiless sovereignty.

* * *

In the realm of dreams, beneath the menacing watch of the *crimson moon*, the ocean takes on an eerie appearance. *Blood waves*, like the sluggish ooze of molasses, *surged* and *clashed* with the forsaken coastline. It was a grotesque paradox, a nightmare etched deeply into the soul of existence.

* * *

Atlas, a man marked by the arrow of time and despair, lies cocooned beneath the disheveled sheets of his bed. His wearied eyes drawn by the pistol resting upon the nightstand, a tempting solution to end his suffering. The stoic man's thoughts resonate in his mind, "I wait and wonder if a second chance will come for humanity. Nothing even happens..."

Beside the pistol, a *compass* necklace rests in silent contemplation. Its slender needle, an unwavering guardian, points west. More thoughts echo within the haunted man's mind, like distant whispers in the empty chambers of his soul. "Then I escape into a dream of my past life."

Atlas closed his eyes and surrendered to the embrace of his memories. He was a vessel adrift the timeline of moments where the past and present intersect.

* * *

A past memory emerged. Atlas, his face smooth and unscarred, lingered in the unchanging solitude of his bed. Moonlight permeated the bedroom through the window, casting an unearthly ethereal luminescence upon the room. His eyes were hypnotized by the crimson moon. A veil of *ash mist* spread everywhere as though the heavens were crying.

Near him, an arm glided across his robust chest. He pivoted as his eyes collided with the *phantom figure* of his wife, *Angelica*, her pregnant condition starkly apparent. Atlas, trembling, extended his fingers to caress her burgeoning belly, his grasp slipping through her translucent form like smoke through the wind.

His eyes remained transfixed by the sinister blood moon. Angelica's ghostly hand graced the rough skin of Atlas's cheek. He shut his eyes and desired the memory of her touch. Like a thread of a dream, her touch escaped him. His soulmate slipped away, forever lost like a shadow in the dead of night.

Atlas was left with a broken heart. A love that dwelled in the abyss of the deepest parts of the soul. The man caught and lost a nostalgic moment of his past life, only conceived in the realm of dreams.

* * *

Returning to the harsh embrace of reality, the hopeful melodies of a piano seeped through the atmosphere. An optimistic song. A faint smile graced the contours of Atlas's face, "That song always gives me hope... for a moment."

Awake and surrounded by the emptiness of his room, Atlas stared directly at an *oxygen tank*. The absence of Angelica lingered. Atlas rose from the bed; his skin exhibited the marks of a world destroyed by the drought. Each line and wrinkle on his face told a story of trials and tribulations caused by the hostile planet. He sat on the edge of the bed, contemplating his bittersweet existence. He was a lost soul searching for thoughts in his mind. "In this world, the simple act of drinking water was a dream."

Atlas approached the wall. He activated a concealed mechanism that summoned a *holographic* projection. A *robodoctor* materialized before him, its artificial intelligence provided a dim ray of medical treatment. The robodoctor methodically examined Atlas's body. The artificial intelligence system's clinical algorithms dissected his condition with a cold, unfeeling precision. Data flickered across the holographic interface, revealing Atlas's state of health. The *robodoctor's* voice, devoid of emotion, cut through the air with clinical precision, "Some dehydration detected." Atlas stared down the robodoctor, unamused by the diagnosis. He grabbed the pistol, concealing it from prying eyes before exiting the room.

Atlas moved through the hallway with extreme focus, his eyes fixed upon the Tyvek-sealed windows that served to be the final defense against the world's toxic air. On the walls hung fading photographs from another time of a family united defiantly against the forces that attempted to obliterate them. The man meticulously reexamined the windows, confirming their resilience. Solar generators not only powered the house's systems but also worked tirelessly to purify carbon dioxide into oxygen. Its advanced *vacuum filtration system* pumped air into the farmhouse's insulated interior. Inside the vacuum filtration system, a complex chemical process called electrolysis and the use of catalysts broke down carbon dioxide, which transformed the molecules into oxygen. The system created breathable air by producing and recycling oxygen. This process was essential for long-duration space missions or closed ecological systems on Earth.

The door creaked open. The living room was bathed in the fiery glow from the inferno outside, the vivid skyline seeping through the boarded windows. Atlas found his daughter, *Charity*, a luminous figure in the subdued atmosphere, captivated by the enchanting tune she was playing. The living room, a library of wisdom, featured shelves that contained books covering the extensive subjects of science, history, and philosophy. Charity, her soul entangled with the music, remained oblivious to her father's arrival. Her favorite childhood memory was sitting at the piano with her mother as they played music together. The daughter's delicate fingers moved gracefully across the piano's keys. A hypnotic connection with the symphony she crafted.

After the sonnet's final note dissipated, Atlas drew near. The proud father spoke, "You're getting better."

Charity turned; her aqua eyes met her father's eyes. "You think so?"

"It's the only sound I look forward to hearing every day…"

"You're just saying that…"

Atlas began his measured retreat, setting a course for the kitchen, "I always tell you the truth. Breakfast?"

Charity's eyes lit up with an infectious enthusiasm, "Can I play one more?"

Atlas's laughter rippled through the room, its warmth a tender sound. "I hope you do you for my sake. I just woke up."

Charity's fingers resumed their elegant dance upon the piano keys. It was another day for the father and daughter, its mysteries unknown, waiting to be unraveled.

The kitchen loomed, an expanse of cold steel. A couple of oxygen tanks rested nearby, silent guardians of survival in the dystopian realm. Shelves sagged under the weight of an endless cache of canned food. It was enough food for a small army during the hardships of survival. Out of nowhere, subtle *tremors* beneath his feet signaled the onset of an earthquake, enough to shake the house. The tremors exponentially gained momentum and intensity, growing in their mighty power.

A geological catastrophe unfolded. The farmhouse shook with malevolent intent. Cans rebelled with frenzied zeal; a metallic chorus chanted discordant hymns of chaos

Urgency coursed through Atlas's being as he darted from the kitchen back into the living room. The tremor grew in magnitude and increased in size—an insane power displayed by Mother Nature herself, a sublime force showcasing its reckoning.

Books tumbled from the shelves as the tremors shook the living room. Charity's hands traced the outline of a metal latch on the trap door. Her movements were deliberate, the wisdom of a seasoned survivor. She unlocked the concealed trap door as the rumble of the tremor continued to grow. Charity's instincts held strong; without hesitation, she yanked the trap door open. A secret passage revealed a ladder that descended into the depths of Earth. An underground bunker. The father and daughter navigated the falling debris with a wordless, unspoken understanding. The farmhouse shook with a wrath of surreal comprehension. Nature was a tyrant, unwavering for anybody who got in her way. Charity climbed down the ladder, entering the subterranean depths. An illuminating lantern embedded in the dirt walls allowed for a safe retreat. Atlas followed his daughter into the underground bunker and slammed the trap door shut behind him. The father and daughter narrowly escaped Earth's fury.

* * *

In years long past, Atlas, his face covered by an oxygen mask, found himself entangled in a nightmarish urban tale. Sirens blared in the background as political monuments and landmarks littered the *dying city*. Their magnificence decayed and slowly evaporated into the wind. Another government empire succumbed to the arrow of time. Lost souls of the dying city stood in line. The humans were gaunt and dehydrated. All gathered and waiting in anticipation of deliverance. Beyond them a *red cross* truck containing the elixir of life, gallons of precious water, made its arrival. This weak oasis of optimism was guarded by *Peace Corp Soldiers*, armored and armed. Tension was thick with adrenaline and encircled this totalitarian state.

A pregnant woman dared to cut the line out of desperation for her unborn child. She begged without mercy, asking for a little more water than offered. The soldier remained silent and unconcerned. His cold heart never wavered from the inhumane response. The soldier's silence during the pregnant woman's plea was met by another intervening soldier, who took a stronger authoritative action. The soldier and pregnant woman screamed at each other, their emotions escalating.

Cruelty was a perilous commodity. Inspired by defiance, the pregnant woman attempted to climb onto the truck's cargo bed. The enraged soldier used his boot as a weapon, kicked a savage blow to her face, and forced her off the truck. She landed hard on the cement, instantly clutching her swollen belly.

A collective gasp from the others rang out in unison as they witnessed the rebellion. Suffering and anger simmered amongst the humans and threatened to boil over in an escalation. The soldiers, sensing the unrest, aimed their guns without hesitation. They directed their lethal intentions onto the restless crowd. During the standoff, a *man* emerged, and fired a loaded AK-47. Bullets upon bullets sprayed into the crowd, killing innocent bystanders along the way. Collateral damage. Plentiful and unapologetic. More panic erupted as desperate humans scattered like leaves in the wind, trampling over each other. Men, women and children of all races and ages were caught in the deadly crossfire. Soldiers nervously gunned down innocent civilians. A savage democide with greater suffering than the World Wars of long ago. Government agencies had turned their back on society, unraveling the thread of trust, unleashing the abyss of violence. The ancient Greek philosophers had always issued warnings about the dangers of imposing excessive control and rigid order upon society. Martial law tightened its stranglehold, exhausting the last vestiges of normalcy from a world that used to be full of hope. Amid the massacre, Atlas retreated, his footsteps guiding him in a desperate drumbeat through the labyrinthine heart of the city. A fugitive escaping the darkness of society. Government empires from the free world collapsed and were forever changed.

* * *

The kitchen walls, observers to the mementos of a family, once held vibrant photographs that were now obscured by layers of dust. Atlas, the protector of those fading memories, embarked on his daily ritual of wiping dust off each one. He continued his janitorial duties of keeping a clean home and attended to fragments of shattered dishes that were scattered across the floor. Slowly but methodically, the father began to restock the canned food items, a repetitive but necessary task. The stoic man's voice, weathered by the weight of the world, broke the silence. "Long ago, our planet surrendered to the drought. The dust never goes away. I'm guilty for allowing my daughter to see this."

Atlas measured out meager portions of uncooked oatmeal into a bowl. He opened a refrigerator that no longer functioned by electricity. Inside was their most prized possession, gallons of water. The man grabbed a gallon and meticulously poured a sparse amount of water into his oatmeal. Liquid intermixes with the dried grains. He scooped up a portion, unimpressed, and gulped it down. "On rare days, when the dust clouds go away, we venture beyond these walls. I understand my daughter's curiosity. I wished for a plan, a hope to share. But the well that sustains us will not last forever. When it runs dry, our home will become our tomb."

The man's eyes drifted to the world outside, camouflaged in the everlasting clouds of dust, a constant reminder of their dystopian reality. Charity interrupted his contemplation, unveiling a charred cellphone. "Look what I found in the attic." The daughter had dreamt of unraveling the mysteries of technology, something she found intriguing.

The father's eyes knew the familiar object all too well. "It was our worst distraction. History repeats itself in different forms, remember that."

The daughter was mesmerized by the cellphone, an ancient artifact of the past, with stories of a world where humans had the power to do almost anything they desired at their fingertips. "Do you think technology was the problem?" she pondered, her aqua eyes fixed on the lifeless device. A man of wisdom who comprehended the deterministic outcome patterns of human behavior within varying environments and under the influence of genetics remained humble in his perspectives.

"Technology gave us both convenience and complexity. The generations before us struggled with its unlimited possibilities."

The daughter sat across from her father, staring outside at the desolate landscape. She pondered her father's words, spoken in a voice as empty as the world they traversed. In the quiet of the dawn, with only the distant howls of wind echoing through the emptiness, she mused on the notion that once, in the past before the world tuned to ash, humans believed in a force they called *electricity*, a mystic current that flowed through wires like veins of some forgotten God. As the hot wind blew through the remains of their dead world, the daughter couldn't help but wonder if there was still a trace of that ancient magic, hidden in the Earth. The daughter spoke candidly, she was a student of knowledge. "In the past, humans thought electricity was magic."

The man, his eyes heavy with insomnia, shuts them; his mind wandered, seeking refuge in a memory. He conjured images of giants, skeletal sentinels extending into the hellish sky. Electricity towers, titans of the past when power crackled through cables like veins pulsing with life. He daydreamed of a time when these metallic behemoths hummed with vitality, orchestrating the symphony of a thriving civilization. His mind, a repository of recollections, replayed scenes of a world where electricity held dominion. A flicker of light at the flip of a switch, the thrumming current coursing through wires, powering the pulse of progress. Those towers, former monuments to human ingenuity, had transformed into relics in the desiccated landscape. The man pondered the temporariness of it all, how the mightiest creations of man could crumble in the face of an unrelenting drought. The old world, used to ablaze energy that these towers conducted, until they were transformed into depleted energy sources. His eyelids, held fast to the vision of a world illuminated. In the quiet recesses of his contemplation, he marveled at the transient dance of electrons, nothing more than a whisper in the fading echoes of a former reality. Atlas lifted his gaze, unfolding the universe within his eyes, and fixed his sight upon Charity. "Electricity was magic, until the world changed."

Charity opened a book and flipped through the pages with excitement; she was a student of information. "Did you know that Earth has witnessed five mass extinctions since the dawn of time? What if, when the drought goes away, a new species emerges?"

The father humbly looked at his daughter, a man of few words but an undeniable logical perspective of their difficult situation. "Without water, it's impossible."

"What if the water returns?"

"For us, it is too late. Eat."

The father's watchful eyes paused upon the swirling dust outside. Charity placed the iPhone on the table and took her seat. Silence intervened between the father and daughter. Both felt the lingering, unexplored topic in the air. Technology was a subject the father rarely spoke about anymore.

"What's on your mind, Dad?"

"Nothing."

"You're sad."

"Why do you think I'm sad?"

The daughter was fully aware of her father's nightly vigils. She always took notice of his silent watch over their home. Atlas was her protector. In the darkness, she occasionally heard his quiet weeping, the sound waves reached her ears like a mournful whisper in the night. "I hear you crying at night."

The man, somewhat of an insomniac in a world that offered no guarantees, found motivation in the unknown of each day. He stared into the dust cloud and replied, "Nightmares. Why are you awake so late?"

The daughter's playfulness shined through as she recognized her father's sense of humor. She replied with a smile. "I didn't think a curfew existed." The father and daughter shared a moment together. Their bond was unbreakable since the day she was born. Their connection ran deeper than most could only dream of having. "It's fine, Dad. I miss Mom, too," the daughter reassured her father. Her words carried her equal weight of their shared loss.

"In this house, it's impossible to forget her."

"Maybe we should consider moving?"

"I heard the real estate market is thriving these days."

They exchanged a fleeting but genuine smile. The father and daughter shared a unique connection. They were best friends, having nobody to trust but each other. "Do you think we might see Mom again?" The question lingered in the air, heavy and filled with uncertainty.

The father's eyes fixed on a distant point, and after a moment of profound silence, he replied, "I don't know, sweetheart. I wish I could give you an answer. Can we talk about something else?" The father wrestled with his inner turmoil, torn between preserving his daughter's faith and the realities of their world. He couldn't strip away any source of hope, especially during the end of days.

The daughter, with a heart full of adventure, had always been an explorer at her core. In her earlier years, she would race around the house in her toy car, a spirited adventurer born in an era where such spirit seemed misplaced. Her optimism shined brightly. Her hope was a rare and precious commodity. "Sure. Can we explore today? Together?"

The father, completely aware of the usual request from his youthful daughter, replied, "Not today. I have a feeling it might rain."

For years, the father and daughter repeated this conversation of potential rain like a modern-day gospel. The possibility of a climate shift was their last hope for humanity. A world reborn became tempting to believe. Stories of resurrections and second comings had woven themselves into the fabric of religion since the dawn of creation. It was an enduring theme that transcended the boundaries of time and culture, offering a rebirth throughout eternity. From his research, the father understood those stories to be fanciful fairytales. The daughter, torn between the tales of miracles and the harsh reality, clung to her carpe diem motto. The prospect of rain seemed more distant than ever.

"It never rains. You need a better excuse," she remarked, her voice tinged with a blend of doubt.

The father, utterly logical, knew supplies were limited. "Exploring a dying world isn't the safest idea."

"I can't live forever in this house."

"Let me think about it."

Charity rolled her eyes. This wasn't the first time she'd been turned down for a possibility of adventure. The resilient daughter spoke with a revered determination. "Why teach me knowledge from those books if I'm going to remain a prisoner in this house? Isn't the point of living to experience life?" The father stood his ground. "Understanding the past is important." Charity innocently pleaded to escape their sanctuary. "I want to see the world with you."

"Finish your breakfast," Atlas said, his patience worn thin. The father rose to his feet, opting to avoid the escalating tension. Conversations like that one had spiraled into conflict in the past. The father preferred to choose the path of least resistance. "We'll see."

Charity, her temper flaring, reluctantly resumed her meal. "You can't protect me forever, Dad." The daughter had a zest for life, curious and naive as youth would allow. She reached for a book and disappeared into its pages. The gravity of their circumstances weighed heavily upon the room. Their separate philosophies for a different life clashed with the undeniable reality they faced. The father left the room, a perpetual conflict within him.

Immersed under the cruel grip of the backyard's afternoon sun, Atlas concealed himself behind a *welder mask*. Black lenses reflected the light of the dynamic star. Wrapped in a trench coat weathered by the harsh touch of nature, he moved like a figure from another world. An oxygen tank, his umbilical cord, hung on his back. He symbolized a working-class superhero. Atlas, his hands covered with construction gloves, grabbed the weathered crank. The pulley's creaks echoed in the air as he began to turn it, one rotation at a time. Atlas watched the wooden bucket descend into the unfathomable abyss of the well. This wasn't his first interaction with the well. Years ago, it saved his life as a young boy. The well continued to perform its duty of carrying out the difficult task of saving the father and daughter's lives by quenching their thirst. There was only so much water left in the world. Each drop was irreplaceable and could be the last. Only meager remnants of water lay hidden beneath the Earth's surface. A modern-day quest for the treasure marked by the elusive X, reminiscent of the days of old when humanity attempted to strike oil or uncover gold.

From the darkness the wooden bucket emerged, a welcoming gift. Fresh, clean water filled to the brim, sloshing back and forth. The water was alive and pure. Atlas took in the miracle and stared at the hypnotic fluid. He knew what they had. He also knew what humans would do if they found out. The man unhooked the bucket. He enjoyed his small but vital victory for survival in this moment. The well was a vessel of hope.

Days had faded into obscurity since humanity's grip on the unruly environment slipped away. Atlas had invested tireless effort in crafting a fortress for his daughter in this desolate nowhere. Buried deep within his consciousness, he understood that chaos lurked on the fringes, driven by the relentless probabilities of their world.

* * *

In a time long past, the boy engaged in a defiant fight against the water's unpredictable fury. His youthful, muscular frame battled with the divine fluid, each frantic movement a desperate plea for deliverance. His screams dissipated underground, intertwined with the depths of the well. Nobody would hear the boy or rescue him. He remained alone, begging for a miracle. His faith was quickly vanishing until a miraculous gift appeared from the deep abyss. From underwater a welder mask emerged, resurrected from its watery grave. The boy reached out and grabbed the welder mask for dear life. Somehow his resilience allowed him to balance precariously on the improbable life raft. His instinctual survival skills allowed him an opportunity to stay above water. The welder mask acted as a buoy, a guardian of safety—his protector under life and death circumstances. From that point on, the boy and welder mask would share a deep connection. The boy defied the relentless undertow, somehow keeping his head above water. After a long fight for survival against nature, the boy was finally able to rest comfortably on the welder mask. He floated gently on the ripples of water. The boy's eyes peered at the opening of the well with a profound sense of gratitude, saved by chance.

*   *   *

The air was a toxic cocktail, reminiscent of the hostile Martian environment. Sulfur and carbon emissions, a noxious veil that suffocated the landscape, made every breath a painful reminder of the Earth's ruined state. Breathing in the polluted air meant embracing a sure path to fatality, as it would course through their lungs like a silent executioner. Atlas towered over a *grave*. His gloved fingers traced the cracks of the tombstone. The man stood in silence, wishing the grave would speak. But it did not. Instead, it remained quiet in the realm of death. A gust of wind rustled the dirt. Swirling dust particles encompassed Atlas. He was surrounded by the tiniest remnants of Earth. Dust particles, the building blocks of matter within the universe, stuck to him. They were his only companions while mourning. A constant reminder of the fading nature of existence. The man would sit by the grave for hours, silently conversing with his departed wife in his mind, sharing every detail of their daughter's daily life. Carved into the grave was a message: *Never lose hope*.

Atlas took his somber journey back to the farmhouse, the bucket of water tightly gripped in his hand. Each step reminded him of the words carved into the grave.

On the distant horizon, a lone *drifter* emerged, their silhouette a ghostly waltz in the dying light of the sun's fading embers. Draped in a tattered cloak and decrepit garments that hung loosely upon their skeletal frame. They wore a *plague doctor* mask, its long beak cast haunting shadows. A relic oxygen tank strapped to their back, a tether to life in a world ravaged by poison. In the dystopian plague doctor's mask—a relic from the dark days of the Black Plague—whispered tales of a grim history when death roamed the world. The beak-shaped mask served as a haunting symbol of the epidemic.

Atlas noticed shadows heading in the direction of the farmhouse. His fatigued eyes locked onto the approaching drifter. Tension continued mounting the closer they got. The drifter's trembling hand outstretched, pleaded for a morsel of mercy, "Please, may I have a sip of water? I haven't had a drop in days."

Atlas gripped the bucket tighter. A decision he wouldn't question twice. Evil lurked across the badlands, and this stranger was no different. The man had learned the hard way never to trust anybody anymore. He stood his ground unwavering in his choice, "Not my problem, stranger."

"I'm not trying to cause trouble."

"Water isn't a gift anymore. I can't just give it away."

"I've walked for miles, praying for a miracle."

"Miracles don't exist…"

"Please, have a heart."

"No…"

The drifter looked at the heavens in deep admiration. "Cruelty has become our currency."

Atlas remained steadfast with his logical reasoning. "In this cruel world, we are left with no one but ourselves to blame."

The drifter collected his thoughts, focusing his undivided attention toward Atlas, "These moments will haunt us… the times we turned our backs on those in need."

Atlas, unimpressed, remained stoic. "May that day of judgement arrive."

The drifter's plague doctor mask looked beyond Atlas, and they became aware of Charity, silently observing them. The stranger embellished this surprise encounter, energized by the unexpected turn of events.

Charity was dressed in a worn trench coat that swirled in the dangerous air. Her face concealed behind a mask, and an oxygen tank strapped securely to her back. The daughter cautiously approached the bucket of water. Atlas attempted to thwart her from grabbing the bucket. "Go back inside, Charity!"

Charity pointed towards the drifter. "Can we help you?"

The drifter took a step forward. "Yes, my dear. May I have a sip of water?"

Atlas glared at the drifter, distrusting the plague doctor. Charity extended her hand towards the bucket, putting her hand on her father's. "Let's just give him some water."

Reluctantly, Atlas released his grip on the bucket, allowing Charity to take control of the water. The father and daughter approached the drifter. The enigmatic figure stood there like a hawk seeking its prey. It was impossible for Atlas to evaluate any semblance of emotion behind the drifter's plague doctor mask. Beneath his trench coat, Atlas produced the pistol he had concealed, maintaining a vigilant aim directed at the stranger. The drifter, sensing the tension, raised trembling hands in a gesture of surrender.

Charity gently put her hands on her father's forearm, pleading for her father to show a sense of mercy. "We're not going to hurt you. Dad, put the gun down." Atlas kept his aim steady with the pistol. "Drink the water."

"Dad, take it easy. He's thirsty!" Charity offered the bucket of water to the drifter. The daughter had compassion. A heart of gold in these unwelcoming times. A kind soul.

The drifter detached his oxygen apparatus. He took a deep breath to avoid the toxic air. Then he consumed the water, guzzling it down as though he'd never drank water before. The bucket emptied in haste. He dropped the bucket onto the arid ground. Its resounding thud echoed through the soundless terrain. Nothing could be heard during those tyrannical times outdoors. Swiftly, the drifter reattached his oxygen apparatus. He breathed in a fresh source of oxygen, securing a steady supply to sustain him in the venomous environment. The drifter's plague doctor mask stared at the well. "Thank you, my guardian angel." He made a creepy gesture of putting his hands in prayer, signaling a gesture of peace and good intent toward the daughter. The drifter pivoted away from the farmhouse, wandering on a path deep across the horizon. The enigmatic figure eventually faded into the imminent sunset. Atlas and Charity remained silent as their eyes focused on the disappearing silhouette that merged with the panoramic horizon.

Underground, deep within the subterranean realm of the bunker, the glow of flickering candles cast shadows. The area was noticeably cooler, another world. Below the surface, dirt and rocks were a place of safety. The environment could withstand punishing solar flares from the sun. The method of surviving underground had been a successful strategy for countless species throughout history. This technique of survival proved fruitful for species of the past. Deep beneath the Earth's surface, creatures endured extinction-level events and thrived in the dark sanctuaries where survival found its way.

Atlas and Charity rival each other across a chessboard. They were mentally engaged in a battle of cleverness. The bunker's thick, dirty walls offered an oasis from the unbearable heat during certain parts of the day. Atlas remained in deep contemplation. The father overlooked all his potential options. His mind adrift after the confrontation with the drifter. "We don't waste our water on humans."

Charity, in the middle of constructing a plan of action with her chess pieces, pondered Atlas's words before she spoke, her voice marked by a firm tone. "Why? We have enough to share."

The father remained certain of the dangers lurking by outsiders. Trust had become a distant memory, a notion abandoned to the winds of betrayal. His face carried the burden of a man driven by a cynical concern. "Our well won't last forever."

Charity's thoughts swirled like a tornado in her psyche. Her aqua eyes darted back and forth, thinking on the turmoil that raged beneath her calm exterior. "Are we going to die?" The looming uncertain future hung like a dark cloud between the father and daughter.

"We have to keep adapting to the environment."

"But what if we can't adapt?"

In his mind, the man contemplated the tenets of Darwinism and acknowledged evolution. It was never guaranteed for any species over time. Atlas paused, his grizzled eyes locked with Charity's in an exchange that spoke volumes. A plea of the reality within their hopeless situation. The father remained wordless and steered clear of the difficult, looming conversation.

"Talk to me, Dad!"

"Thinking bad thoughts is never a good idea."

The daughter, on the verge of frustration, leaned forward. "I want to fight for a better future."

The father remained honest. "There is no future."

Charity had learned about ancient cultures that rebelled against the climate catastrophe. Their love and determination for the world were a wellspring of inspiration for her in these trying times. "I don't believe you. Across history, humanity confronted the impossible and prevailed. Can you really give up hope?" Fortune and failure, like two sides of a coin.

The father, well-versed in scientific literature, understood that they were not destined for fortune; failure seemed to be the only option. With a heavy heart, he spoke the harsh truth, "The damage caused to our planet is irreversible."

Charity held profound respect for her father's knowledge and the scientific perspective he offered. But, deep within her, she had hope for humanity and whispered, "We're not going to become extinct."

The father remained silent. He knew nothing would come out of honesty. His philosophy in life was that sometimes saying nothing opposed to something was the best approach. Quietness spread across the air. A tranquil moment amidst the conflict. Charity leaned in; her unwavering aqua eyes focused upon the candle's flame. She closed her eyes and made a wish to herself. The daughter would not dare speak about her wish out loud; she knew it would jinx the opportunity of it coming true. With a soft exhale, Charity extinguished the candle's fragile light, plunging their bunker into darkness.

The living room was cloaked in the trembling glow of candlelight. Shadows danced with the ghosts of a world in its death march. Atlas, submerged by the disorder surrounding their existence, creaked back and forth in a rocking chair. His eyes wandered to the window. The man watched the night as though life would appear. All he saw was an inhospitable world on the brink of its own expiration. A departed world that had no chance of a second chance. Better days were behind them.

These days, civilizations were shepherds of their own destruction. Agriculture no longer existed. The animal kingdom was erased. Clean air was a distant memory from the ancient world—the past of this dying world. The dance of oxygen molecules, long ago held as life's cherished breath, until they surrendered to the jaws of the runaway greenhouse's fiery inferno. With each quiver and shiver, they intertwined with carbon, creating a tale eternally etched in the winds of change. The cruel alchemy of life's silent exhalation was now the song of carbon dioxide's unstoppable embrace.

This was a time of night when dark thoughts wore on the man. Atlas reached for the sweet poison of alcohol. These days he never even bothered grabbing a glass and drank straight from the bottle. He drank heavily. Tears welled his eyes. The man knew they were on borrowed time. The combination of limited water and oxygen were issues beyond his control. All he could do was wait until it was their time to either suffocate or dehydrate. He read about the past world, where humans could live effortlessly in nature, enjoying their sacred planet. Oceans and forests seemed like dreams of an afterlife straight from the pages he'd scoured—tales written on brittle paper, echoing in the quiet chambers of his mind. Magic, it sounded, in a world that had grown lean on such wondrous things, where the fading echoes of the old stories had turned to rumors in the wind.

Nature, a God in the old world, was now the devil. As he continued to drink, a relentless sound entered his psyche as he began to hallucinate. The sound of *ocean waves* crashing against distant shores, serene and tranquil. The man had never seen an ocean before, but he read about it. All he could do was dream about what it could be to try to find an ounce of peace in his weary soul. The rocking chair's steady hypnotic rhythm combined with his drowsy state of consciousness lured him into the arms of a peaceful sleep.

A sudden blaze of *bright lights* fractured the moment. Their illuminating brilliance, a distant beacon. The lights were moving closer to the farmhouse with an unstoppable purpose. Atlas's eyes felt the rays of photons, packets of light particles hitting his eyelids, jarring him awake. The man stared into the bright lights and squinted as he sought salvation in their radiance.

His senses kicked in his adrenaline. He snapped back to an awake state. Peaceful sleep was a privilege these days and this wasn't the time. The man got up from the rocking chair and navigated his way towards the concealed hatch in the floor. His hand clutched the handle and wrenched the door open. "Wake up! Get dressed, gather all you can!"

Charity awoke from her dreams. Her father's voice, a shrill wake-up call, sliced through the mysticism of sleep. In that instant, she understood the gravity of their situation. The daughter scrambled to dress herself in her protective attire. Time became an urgent matter as the seconds ticked away. She had never seen her father act this way before and knew this was something different. Nerves coursed through her, spreading from head to toe like an electric current.

In the fragile cocoon of dawn, Atlas stepped forth onto the porch, cloaked in the armor of a working-class superhero. The welder's mask veiled his face. He stood fearless, shotgun in hand. The man, a loyal warrior, an embodiment of resilience.

From the murky depths of early morning, a menacing *tank* emerged, its metallic frame glistened ominously as it closed the distance to the farmhouse. The tank, a relic from distant wars of the past, had once rumbled across battlefields in the crucible of World War I and II. The steel behemoth was a reminder of the horrors that had scarred the world during a bygone era. The ancient vehicle served as a catalyst, a weapon of mass destruction in pursuit of the well. Slowly the tank imposed its menacing presence. The wheels churned in rhythmic precision, like the intricate cogs of a perfectly synchronized clock. Each revolution a flawless symphony of machinery in motion. With an abrupt halt, the tank stopped a couple hundred yards away from the farmhouse.

A gang of armed *plague doctors* exited from its structure. Each of them clutched a firearm. Among the tribe of debauchery, the drifter, their leader, led the way. He knew the rarity of the well was a gift from God, though the existence of a higher power remained hypothetical. The drifter's rasping voice spoke. "The water belongs to us!"

Atlas raised his shotgun as conflict and intensity weaved through the air. Charity quickly joined her father's side. "Take cover!" The daughter ducked behind the shield of her father in the middle of the encroaching attack. The sun's departure painted the sky with fiery hues, setting the stage for the battle over water.

An orchestra of *gunshots erupted.* The avalanche of bullets created a crescendo of violence and reverberated across the salt flatlands. Silence became history, only warfare was heard. Atlas and the plague doctor gang engaged in a savage exchange of fire, their bullets escalating a deafening discharge. The porch became an arena of death. Amidst the hurricane of violence, Atlas moved back and forth dodging bullets. The daughter stayed close behind her father, whose body moved with an athletic precision borne of absolute necessity. He positioned himself as a defensive wall, his body a shield against the bullets as he protected his daughter. Bullets ripped into his tattered trench coat but had no effect. A bulletproof vest was his safeguard.

Charity noticed the gang of plague doctors were edging closer to the farmhouse. The father and daughter were outnumbered, and time remained of the essence. "I'll gather what we need!" Brave and resilient, Charity vanished into the farmhouse. Her mission was clear: Grab all the water and oxygen she could carry. Atlas persisted, moving in a deadly dance with the plague doctors, his gunfire providing cover for Charity.

Back in the farmhouse, Charity's instincts propelled her towards the kitchen. She darted with the grace of a hunted creature. Bullets penetrated the walls, ripping through boarded windows. Steel bullets tore through the wood with ease. Debris and wood scattered like wild spirits, torn apart by the fury of the bullets' savage downpour of lead. Charity dove to the ground, seeking refuge behind furniture. She waited until the warfare calmed down. Relentless bullets continued to sing death's desire and came perilously close while she huddled behind a couch. Every nerve in her being tensed. The ambush grew fiercer by the second. The daughter made a move for the kitchen, putting herself in the deadly crossfire. She dodged and weaved and barely avoided any harm to her body. The daughter harbored a resolve etched by time and sharpened by the cruel edge of loss. Her mind and body had been honed over seasons; a preparation set in motion when the world grew cold with her mother's departure.

Her youthful energy was euphoric; she had never encountered the outside world. The daughter's entire life had been hidden from the reality of the apocalypse. All she ever did was read books about the end of days. This challenge threw her into the heat of battle without warning. Her instincts were impressive. She remained confident with her prowess despite the army of bullets. Charity moved with the quiet intent of a scavenger. She entered the kitchen and assembled a collection of water bottles and canned food, tossing them into a satchel. A pair of oxygen tanks joined their supplies. She tossed the satchel and oxygen tanks over her shoulder. It was quite a load but manageable. The daughter had genetically inherited her father's fighting strength.

An intense *crack* pervaded the air. Wooden boards on the farmhouse splintered and shattered under the nonstop assault of a plague doctor wielding a *flamethrower*. This weapon of annihilation discharged its incendiary wrath, birthing an inferno that consumed the kitchen.

Charity maintained her nimbleness from the unpredictable nature of the attack. Massive flames consumed the kitchen. The daughter navigated past the voracious flames with the grace of a ballerina. Each step was a gamble in the game of survival. In the trenches of the hellish conflagration, she emerged unscathed, reaffirmed by the fickle hand of fate. Lugging her supplies, Charity reentered the warzone on the front porch.

Atlas remained unshakable amidst the storm. He placed his body between the blitz of bullets and Charity. He would go to the end of Earth to protect his precious daughter. His shield of silence, the bulletproof vest, continued to absorb the deadly gunfire.

The drifter stepped forward, demented, and raging mad. "Are you prepared for your rebirth!?" The tank, a behemoth of innovation, pivoted with precision. Its *cannon rotated*, creating a cold calculation, and aligning its sights squarely upon the farmhouse.

Atlas noticed the detrimental event about to unfold before his eyes. He turned to his daughter. "*Run!*" The father and daughter rushed away from the porch, running through the dangerous open space of the salt flatlands. Bullets ricocheted close to them, creating mists of white salt in the air. In one seamless motion, Atlas aimed his shotgun while running, unleashing rapid fire that cut down a couple of plague doctors as they scrambled in retreat toward the waiting Tesla. The father hung back and provided cover for Charity, allowing her to escape the encounter. She ran as fast as she could, carrying all the supplies she had gathered. The weight of the objects made it challenging, but her willpower pushed her physically to the limits. Their existence hung by a slender thread. The nonstop gunfire echoed through the badlands, a violent soundtrack accompanying their frantic escape toward their getaway.

A thunderous *kaboom* resounded as the tank released a *devastating round*. The farmhouse decimated, a *colossal explosion*. Their refuge of survival was gone forever, the home of memories reduced to piles of rubble. Atlas aimed his shotgun at the plague doctors, firing a barrage of bullets in their direction. Each shot was a passionate action for survival. The sound of shotgun rounds filled the air, claiming the lives of more plague doctors.

Charity urgently entered the driver's seat. She overlooked the control panel as her fingers navigated the labyrinth of buttons and screens. Inside the Tesla, a familiar routine unfolded. The hum of the vehicle's systems and the soft glow of controls illuminated the interior. The daughter had rehearsed those silent rituals of ignition and emergency escape with the Tesla. Her vigilance was quite impressive in the face of an unseen world. Unseen it was, but the call when it came found her poised to leap into the unknown. A sense of readiness forged in her soul. She cast anxious glances over her shoulder, her impatience tangible as she awaited her father's return. The echoes of the current gunfight lingered in the air, a haunting sound of violence. "Dad, we can't wait much longer!"

A series of gunshots raced past Atlas; the overpowering bombardment of ammunition left him hopelessly outmatched. Faced with no other recourse, he ran away from the pandemonium. The father's steps quickened, his heart pounding in his chest. He knew they had to escape before their pursuers overwhelmed them. The father ran faster, his feet pounding the cracked Earth. Atlas dove into the passenger seat and avoided bullets that whizzed perilously close to the Tesla. The world outside blurred into a chaotic frenzy of ferocity.

"Drive!"

"I don't know how!"

"Here!"

Atlas forced Charity's quivering foot to the gas pedal. The Tesla moved suddenly *backward*, leaving behind the well and the grave—symbols of a past they had to let go. Charity's restless spirit guided the Tesla in a backwards dance, evading the oncoming enemy fire. Each maneuver was a desperate gambit in a world where danger lurked at every crossroad.

The tank discharged another *catastrophic round*, barely missing the Tesla, catapulting *debris* into the turbulent sky. Bullets, like angry wasps, reflected off the Tesla's bulletproof frame. Atlas leaned out of the passenger window, shotgun in hand, and took aim. Each shot fired a prayer to answer the predatory advance of the ruthless plague doctors.

In a sudden, shrieking halt, the Tesla executed a razor-edged turn, transitioning smoothly from *reverse* to *forward*. The Tesla accelerated with astonishing speed. They departed, leaving a haunting canvas of the aftermath. A skirmish they emerged victorious from now carried the scars of a war they had lost. The Tesla continued to distance itself from the farmhouse. Atlas reentered the vehicle from the window.

His eyes looked at where the farmhouse once stood, now erased from the face of the Earth. "We have to start over."

Charity nodded, her gaze steadfast, fixed on the unknown path ahead. A road burdened with uncertainty. An unknown landscape where their own survival would fight against all odds. Only a miracle could guide them to safety. The father and daughter had no choice but to follow the road, searching for hope.

If you do not take an interest in the affairs of your government, then you are doomed to live under the rule of fools.
Plato

It is not the strongest of the species that survive, nor the most intelligent, but the one most responsive to change.
Charles Darwin

SURVIVE

*Earth provides enough to satisfy every man's need
but not every man's greed.*
Gandhi

* * *

An ancient city stood, a former institution of thriving human laws and regulations. Their politics crumbled; a forgotten construct flawed from the beginning. Now it stood as an evocative testimony to the collapse of civilization. The streets were crowded with motionless traffic. Solar flares had rained chaos upon the world. Transportation, the pulse of civilization, became crippled in the aftermath—a river of immobile abandoned automobiles remained. The mighty engines of progress had fallen silent, their mechanical parts stilled by the unaccountable wrath of the cosmos. No longer did the roads hum with the seamless rhythm of tires on asphalt, nor did the skies sing with the majestic engineering of planes. In the quietness of this new age, humanity faced a harsh truth: The atmosphere, giver of life, had become a judge of destiny, and it cared not for the ambitions of humanity.

The air had been rendered frail by the unchecked proliferation of greenhouse gases—nothing more than a whisper in the face of impending ruin. Humanity's suffocating atmosphere, where every breath was a battle, became the norm. *Protestors* moved with dignified determination. Oxygen tanks and masks were their lifelines in this asphyxiating world. Each step they took reverberated through the dystopian city. A haunting pulse of resistance against the stranglehold grip of the environment choked their spirits. With their faces hidden behind masks, they were nameless, voiceless. The humans marched; their footsteps spoke of a firm purpose. Protestors pleaded to the heavens for a future where the air wasn't a toxic enemy but a source of life again.

Atlas's voice spoke from a deep place of reflection. "Our world was condemned by the arrogance of its leaders. They dismissed the cries for help, trapped by their pursuit of profit."

In the Middle East, where the overabundance of greenhouse gases continued its role as tormentor, water wars raged like wildfires. Nations engaged with brutality and savagery. Each droplet of water was an idolized prize in a world desiccated by scarcity. The land, rich with stories of ancient civilizations, was now on the brink of genocide. A different saga emerged, forcing water to become the most coveted currency. The world felt like a surreal dream—an eternal nightmare of death and suffering. Water wars cast a shadow over the land and its drought-stricken inhabitants. In the heart of the ancient desert, water grew as rare as the enigmatic verses of the Dead Sea Scrolls themselves.

Intervening the corruption corridors of power, politicians were entangled in their agendas. They clutched tightly to the reins of scientific progress. Their decisions withheld the pursuit of innovation and discovery. Within the hallow halls of Congress, the debate over the approaching climate catastrophe raged on, a tempest of impassioned voices. The only deal achieved was a resounding agreement to disagree, leaving progress forever lost in the gathering storm. Politicians deprived science of the vital resources and grants required to explore sustainable solutions. The Paris Climate Agreement papers were no less significant than ancient scrolls and drifted like tumbleweeds down the vacant hallways of the Senate. Their inked promises lost in the wind of indifference. The world approached the precipice of environmental collapse. Humanity's foreseen stubbornness cast a spell over the hopes of a solution. The pursuit of knowledge battled against political schemes and determined the fate of generations to come.

Innocent forests, the heartbeat of life, surrendered to the furious fury of unchecked forest fires. These voracious flames, like ravenous demons, devoured all in its path. All that remained were charred remnants of an apocalyptic world. The crackling of burning wood created a mournful elegy for nature. A requiem for the beauty and life that had been lost to the inferno. In this mass destruction, the Earth seemed to weep. The planet's tears joined the ashes of a world forever altered. Atlas's voice registered with concern. "Our existence encountered the unpredictability of nature."

The ocean waters, a former home for the cradle of creation, were overtaken by oil. Countless marine species suffocated to death, smothered in fossil fuels. Waves, carried by the demise of an ecological tragedy, washed ashore the lifeless bodies of oceanic creatures. Their simplistic crime? Inhabiting a world spoiled by the careless hand of humanity. Within this watery graveyard, the world was forever altered by the production of pollution. The sea was consumed by oil and nuclear waste, an abyss where the sins of mankind mingled with the depths. During the crusade of humanity's energy era, the ocean simmered with unchecked rage and absorbed heat equivalent to the energy of five submerged atomic bombs exploding every second, 24 hours a day. Atlas's voice carried an unspoken truth. "The air we once took for granted haunts every breath we take."

Amid the stark desolation of the coastline, an unsettling sight of lifeless fish washed upon shore—a silent testimony to a monumental environmental collapse. The Pacific trash vortex was an expanding graveyard of synthetic refuse. A disgusting manifestation of excess, spread like a cancer across the waters, choked the life from the ocean. Overconsumption of goods was the dire consequence of unchecked greed. Plastic reached its insatiable coils across the ocean, entrapping unsuspecting inhabitants of the deep. Under the ash skies of a world tormented by indifference, the task of recycling proved itself a Sisyphean struggle, its efforts dwarfed by the magnitude of the climate catastrophe.

Mankind, like Sisyphus, found themselves forever condemned to push the boulder of their own environmental hubris up the steep mountain, an eternal cycle of endless conversations led towards no viable solutions.

Desperation reigned supreme within the megalopolis. The streets were a theater of poverty. The city's troubled citizens stood in endless lines that snaked through the heart of the concrete jungle. Each person tightly clutched a bucket, with the hopes of receiving water in this wasteland, their feet restrained to pavement from the oppressive heat. The scorching concrete beneath their feet became so intense it seemed to melt their shoes. "We may be the last to witness this tragedy. Water, the crucible of our existence, evaporated into the realm of fading memories," Atlas continued, his voice filled with emotion. The pale blue dot, our home, has transformed into a nightmare, a realm unrecognizable from the vibrant planet it once was.

*   *   *

The Tesla journeyed across the everlasting expanse of dreary terrain. An unending panorama of havoc unfurled in all directions. The forsaken Earth had undergone a metamorphosis into an alien landscape. A realm where life's footprints had long been expunged. Covering this desolate canvas were the shattered mementos of satellites. Metallic corpses twisted and warped. Fragments of human innovation represented a phantasmic apparition. A paradoxical reminder of another era reduced to an echo of its former glory. When satellites wandered the universe, they offered glimpses of Earth's own destiny. They provided revelations of the future, which became forgotten scriptures, never finding their place in the ancient world's collective consciousness.

The vivid green and blue that embellished Earth had vanished into oblivion and was now replaced by a brown and gray palette of monochrome bleakness. A dreamlike image that showcased evidence for the cruel absence of water. The Tesla continued onward, its wheels kicking up dust and dirt. Each passing mile served as confirmation of a world bled dry of its most precious resource.

Atlas had a deadpan stare across the inhospitable world. He steered the Tesla through the treacherous landscape, the two of them momentarily freed from the confines of their masks. The father's eyes, etched with the wounds of time, caught a glimmer of disappointment reflected in Charity's eyes as she absorbed the desolate tableau surrounding them. Her youthful innocence seemed to fade, eclipsed by the harshness of their reality. The father, messenger of prophecies about the apocalyptic Earth, had cautioned his daughter. In the end, a single image painted a more vivid tale than a thousand words ever could.

"It wasn't always like this, you know." Charity's mind wandered back to her youth, to the time when her mother would sit her down and spin tales of ancient Earth. "Mom used to tell me stories of a blue world."

"It was. A long time ago…" The father's words trailed off; they were echoes from a fading species.

"You can close your eyes…"

"I want to see it all…" Her aqua eyes focused on a venomous fog of toxic gas that spread in every direction in the sky—an insidious veil that smothered every surface in its path.

Along the road, deserted and rusted vehicles decayed away into the rocky ground, relics from different eras. Mounds of *human skeletons* were stacked upon each other. The bones were a soul-stirring monument to the unending arrow of extermination for humanity. In this dystopian age, humanity's obsessions resembled a trail similar to the rust-red lands of Mars—a realm envisioned in the olden days when humans were explorers and etched their will upon an unforgiving frontier. Earth, in its transformation, resembled Mars. It was not the crimson orb of legend but rather the rugged face of the brown planet. The soul of the world had a graveyard of archaeological discovery and contained secrets of countless eras buried in the layers of its ancient ground.

The Tesla drove slowly; both father and daughter took notice of the taboo imagery of skeletons scattered across the road. Dozens of skeletons represented, in the end, the majority of humanity who, driven by a relentless spirit, chose the open road over the confines of shelter. They preferred to venture into the unknown with a dwindling supply of water and oxygen. For, at its core, humanity had always been an adventure, a restless quest at the core of its existence. The texture of mountains was etched in time and stood strong.

Rocks, the Earth's ancient sentinels, were the first to emerge and would endure until the end of their fading world. Beauty and ugliness were intertwined in eerie harmony. The ancient rocks were witness to the epic journey of humanity, a transformation that unfolded across eons. From the primordial soup to civilizations, spanning billions of years across the timeline.

"Perseverance for mankind is over…"

"Forgive us, Earth…"

Charity's fingers found comfort in the cool touch of the windowpane within the Tesla. The vehicle's robust cooling system shielded them from the hostility of the outside world. The daughter's aqua-colored eyes filled with sorrow and wonder. Her curious mind raced as she comprehended the planet she inhabited.

Oil derricks loomed over the landscape like lookout towers. Their monolithic figures cast ominous shadows upon the barren oil field. The towering derricks were steel giants, monuments to a technological metamorphosis that ushered humanity out of the modern era into the furnace of the Industrial Revolution. Progress forged a new destiny from the smoldering fires of innovation. Carved into the parched, fractured Earth, an eerie message surfaced like a ghostly oracle: *Thank you humanity for our extinction.*

Charity looked away, ashamed. Atlas observed the profound impact the otherworldly scenery had on his daughter. He began to reflect aloud, his words measured and contemplative. "As a species, we were always quick to point fingers. We only change when disaster comes near us. This time, we hesitated for too long."

The daughter, her mind steeped in tales of time's enigma, had delved deep into the mysteries of time travel, often dreaming of what an alternate era might have to offer. "I wish," she sighed, "I could journey through time, to see this place when it was happy."

The scholarly father, riddled with information, had to tell her the sad truth. Amidst his extended repertoire of reading, he had always discerned a single unending thread marked by the ever-present diversity of human beings—a thread that represented their complexity and conflicts. "It was," he pondered with a heavy heart, "a story that was never truly happy."

Charity, her nature inclined towards thoughtful contemplation, fixed her mind upon her father. "What do you mean?" she inquired, her curiosity apparent.

One of the uncomfortable truths that the father knew was the revelation of why humanity had crumbled in the middle of its darkest hours. "We lost our way," he confessed. "We forgot the art of unity, how to fix the breaks and bridge our differences. People didn't listen, and by the time we understood the world was changing, it was already too late. Our planet was drained dry." The road stretched seemingly to infinity, its forlorn path accentuated by the waning sun, casting mortality.

*　*　*

Water molecules, the creators of our planet, were weakened in the unforgiving trap of the runaway greenhouse effect. Bound by the dance of covalent bonds, which had evolved through epochs, they were sentenced to a defying transformation. As the heat enveloped them, their fragile connections frayed and unraveled like the ancient threads of fate. These molecules ascended reluctantly, as if thrust upon a sacrificial altar into the heavens, where they dissipated into a void of nothingness. Their collective sacrifice marked the quiet tragedy of a world forsaken by its own existence. A requiem for the lost covenant between Earth and its most cherished element.

*　*　*

The Tesla parked in a valley of a rugged sea of mountains. The summit, their stony faces weathered by time, carried by the distant whispers of wind. Nature, in her timeless existence, had been engaged in an eternal conversation with herself. She whispered secrets to the wind and scribed them upon the stones. She murmured in the rustle of leaves and the flow of rivers. Her voice was a symphony of ages; a language older than the oldest of tongues. From the primordial chaos to the delicate balance of ecosystems, she spun her narrative, composing a saga of life and death, of chaos and order, where each being played a part in the cosmic stage of existence. She was the author of an epic story, written not on paper but etched in a narrative throughout spacetime for eternity. The daughter exited the vehicle and looked over the daunting mountains. Charity's eyes were entranced by the world's transformation. The daughter voiced her opinion of disbelief. "It's hard to believe it's all gone."

Atlas continued the methodical task of changing the batteries, his hands moving with practiced precision. They had a limited supply. The father knew this and was quickly analyzing a plan of action in his mind. Charity remained immersed in her otherworldly experience, an encounter that tugged at her soul. While books imparted their wisdom, they could only provide a limited glimpse of the full spectrum of life's lessons. It was through living life to its fullest potential that one could truly grasp the depth of knowledge and gain a profound perspective on the world.

"Maybe a miracle could still happen?" The father, a staunch believer in ontological realism, often voiced a stark truth in the dim corners of their world.

"There are no miracles left in this world." His conviction ran deep as he beheld the truth through eyes unclouded by delusions, where the extraordinary had been eclipsed by time. Even the most wondrous of mysteries had surrendered to the mundane.

The daughter, her heart drawn to the concept of evolution and the boundless possibilities it held, found hope in the idea that change was an invincible force, a tide that could reshape and improve the world over time. Her faith in the promise of evolution became her guiding light. "Evolution," she mused, "teaches us that change is a current, a force woven into life. Do you not believe that, as a species, we can have another transformation? Earth will not stay like this forever. Things can change for the better." In the hushed stillness of the air, words were mute to the profound gravity of the moment. Optimism and pessimism waged their silent war. The daughter, determined, fought to maintain her faith. In this world of fading hope, her belief remained a spark against the darkness.

Atlas finished switching out the battery and joined his daughter. They absorbed the stark beauty of the mountains. Charity's eyes welled with tears. She wandered away from her father, hypnotically pulled by the sheer horror of Earth and remained completely speechless. Her aqua eyes fixated on the dystopian world. It felt like a dream to her, something surreal and distant, as if it wasn't real at all. "It's just not fair..."

Atlas knew wisdom was a dwindling currency. He sensed the urgency of the moment, understanding that whatever life lesson he could impart to his daughter would serve as the compass for their shared journey. "You're right; life rarely is fair." His voice was a well-worn testament to the trials of life.

"No more helping people. Humanity has forgotten the difference between right and wrong." Charity, her heart a home for enduring hope, held onto the prayer for humanity. In the depths of her being, she maintained a belief that good resided within the soul of every human being. A spark obscured by the shadows of the world but could never truly be extinguished.

"I can't accept that everyone is bad," she said.

"We live in a world where darkness wins. Each day is a struggle," the father imparted, his words a blend of poetic wisdom and stark reality. "But we never surrender, no matter the odds. You must understand all this... I won't be here forever to tell you things." His voice, like that of a sage, resonated with an irrefutable clarity.

The daughter's emotions, like a sudden arrow released from a bow, struck her heart. The thought of losing her father gripped her youthful soul with terror. "Promise me," her voice quivered, "promise that you'll never leave me behind."

In a moment of fear, Charity pushed her father away. It was the first time she had ever heard him talk about the possibility of his own death. The idea of her father dying was something she couldn't bear to think about. Atlas tenderly embraced his daughter, holding her close in a heartfelt hug. "I'm not going anywhere..." In that instant, a wordless bond formed. An unspoken understanding that affirmed their deep love for each other, in a world that had veered so far from its former course.

*   *   *

Within the dream realm, candlelight casts an exquisite glow upon the bathroom. Angelica, her face aglow with an inner radiance, reclined gracefully in the bathtub. Atlas sat perched on a stool by the tub, his eyes locked on a speech heard in the distance. The television, a lone voice in the darkness, murmured the news, its anchor's sad voice filled the air with an unmistakable sense of looming catastrophe. "The United Nations has withdrawn from the Humanitarian Act for Earth…"

Suddenly, the television screen goes dark. Angelica extended her elegant hand, offering the compass necklace. "Take this. Keep it safe. It'll be your guide after I'm gone."

Atlas accepted the necklace as his trembling fingers traced the detailed outline of the compass pendant. Tears welled in his eyes. "I can't lose you again. Please, don't leave me."

Angelica gathered her thoughts and produced a delicate smile. "Look after our daughter. Protect her. The world is changing, and you must fight for her future." Atlas watched in distress as Angelica sunk underwater. Panic grabbed him as he desperately splashed the water, searching for any sign of her. A lonely moment stretched on, extending what seemed like eternity. There was nothing but a profound silence, a void of any trace of Angelica. She slipped away in the underworld, vanished into the mystifying depths of the unknown—a realm that remained concealed in mystery, uncertain of its own existence. Atlas collapsed to his knees and clutched the compass necklace tightly. His memento of the love they shared. The man stared at the vacant bathtub and watched water ripples mirror his grieving reflection.

He hung his head in shame, an enormous loss that forever marked his soul.

* * *

Within the calmness of the bank's vault, Charity's gloved fingers skillfully maneuver through stacks of money. These material vestiges were once symbols of boundless wealth. The daughter had read about money. She understood it as a bargaining system of trust between civilizations. A trust that became forever lost after the environmental collapse. All that remained was intricate mazes of currency. The paper object represented cryptic patterns of a world long ago, where billions and trillions held immense meaning and power.

Atlas seized handfuls of bills and stuffed them into a duffel bag with a sense of purpose. The father had long grasped the allure of extreme wealth and the danger it posed to the foundation of civilization. To him, currency had always been a tool of governmental control, a sneaky force that conquered humanity.

Charity, beside him, studied the money with curiosity in her eyes. Her fingers gently traced the faded contours of a world that had decayed into nothingness, one bill at a time. "It's strange how something that was once so important has become useless. What are we doing with all this money?"

Atlas continued to fill the duffel bag with obsolete cash. "It burns good. It'll keep us warm."

Charity examined a crumpled hundred-dollar bill, her expression contemplative. "Wasn't this what people always fought over?" Atlas gazed upon the paper devil, a twisted creation born from a forgotten world. Money, a symbol of bureaucracy, had shriveled into a paradoxical parody of its former self. The numbers etched upon its surface were a testament to the greed of civilization. Nothing more than a discordance of forgotten laws and regulations.

Atlas's eyes, haunted, lingered on the currency relic, a harbinger that killed Mother Nature. "People used to spend their entire lives in pursuit of money, making sacrifices, and at times, hurting others in their pursuit of greed. And now, it's just paper, worthless."

Charity's thoughts drifted away from the money and focused back on the improbable journey they were embarking on. "Where are we headed, Dad?"

"To the coast?"

"Why all the way out there?"

Atlas's mind flickered like a dying flame, casting fragmented memories upon the dark canvas of his thoughts. Each memory was like grains of sand that slipped through his clutched fingers. Lost but not forgotten, a moment in time that he would never forget until the day he died.

* * *

Atlas and Angelica, encased in their protective survival suits, found a moment of reflection during the ash flake storm. An ancient *lighthouse* stood proud and tall, unbroken amid the end of days that engulfed their world. The lighthouse contained a semblance of hope in the middle of a world torn apart by catastrophe.

They pressed forward along the pier, a haunting spectacle materialized before their eyes. A former vibrant fairground, blanketed in a thick veil of dust. Ash blanketed the essence of this place, the final layer atop a cake of existence. A phantasmagorical vision of destruction. The Ferris wheel emitted mournful creaks in the breeze. Stuffed animals, once coveted prizes, remained undisturbed, suspended in a timeless slumber. In unison, Atlas and Angelica continued their journey along the pier, inching ever nearer to its daunting edge. They lingered there in an uncanny silence, their gazes transfixed on the surreal tableau that engulfed them, witnessing the oceanic world irreversibly transformed.

* * *

Atlas completed the task of stuffing the duffel bag, each crumpled bill added to the growing challenge that lay ahead. "There's a lighthouse. It could be our new home. And… the beaches offer us the best chance of finding water…"

Charity's youthful eyes widened with curiosity, her face etched with questions. "Aren't the oceans dangerous?" Atlas stared into the abyss of the money bag, his mind wandering towards the treacherous journey.

"It's a risk we must take. Water is our only lifeline. Remember, the money is just for burning. It can't buy clean air or restore what's lost."

Charity swiftly pocketed the remaining bills, a sense of urgency in her movements. She nodded as her young face reflected the gravity of their predicament. She held onto her discipline of knowledge, unwavering in her pursuit, always learning, regardless of the truths that might unfold. "All this money. It feels meaningless now."

The father, a human of understanding in her world, spoke with a mortal man's wisdom. "Greed destroys all…"

Atlas walked away from the bank and never glanced back. Charity allowed her eyes to linger a moment longer, a final contemplative look at the abandoned trillions they were leaving behind. The daughter briefly surrendered to a daydream and imagined the unfamiliar sensation of being a trillionaire in a world she had never known, a world untouched by the apocalypse. A world where the boundaries of possibility seemed boundless. Shaking off the alluring thought, she turned her back on the illusion of infinite wealth, knowing that in their world, it was a mirage too fragile to hold onto. A philosophical symbol of a capitalist world gone adrift in the history of time.

*   *   *

A heavy shroud of smoke and ash hung over the pristine sky. The world was gripped by a darkness cast by the towering chimneys. They were sinister titans of the fossil fuel industry. The world had changed, and not for the better. In the nucleus of the wretched world, vestiges of coal-fired power plants belched forth plumes of thick, acrid smoke, and the rhythmic thumping of machinery echoed.

Where the mighty waterfalls of Niagara Falls rumbled, there now only existed an echoing void, a silent abyss of nothingness. The water had vanished. Only the dramatic cliff and the waterless riverbed remained. The termination of nature.

In the former majestic Cave of Crystals in Naica, Mexico, perfect geometric admiration dissolved under the scorching heat. Every droplet fell from the degenerating structures and carried tears from the past. The magnificence of this subterranean realm was erased, forever lost like a breath in a breeze.

The Xiaolangdi Dam in China, a pillar to human engineering and supremacy, transformed into a foregone relic due to the nefariously undefeated arrow of time. Waters that flowed freely through its gates evaporated, leaving the unique architecture structure deteriorating, submitting to the jaws of Earth.

In South Africa, uninhabited farmlands, once flourishing with food crops such as rice, wheat, barley, oats, fruits, and vegetables, conceded defeat from the lack of fermentation. The ungodly drought reduced the area to arid dust. Crops withered and obliterated. The cradle of civilization a rumor of ages long ago.

Dallol, Ethiopia, an observer to rocks transformed into surreal forms of nature. The brown and gray rocks of prior form turned a corner in their evolutionary trajectory. They now radiated a vibrant spectrum of colors. Their enchanting beauty contradicted the unwelcoming environment. Acidic hot springs contained similar pH levels of battery acid. Hydrothermal vents and geysers were surrounded by a foreign landscape with colors of vibrant yellows, greens, and oranges. The absence of oxygen condemned existence into a waning vestige.

* * *

The Tesla navigated through an *ash storm*. From the heavens an ominous bombardment of gray ashes descended, a mournful precipitation that seemed to weep for the world's irreversible decay. The storm swept across like remnants of a colossal cremation event, as if the Earth had been turned into a requiem. The ash particles pirouette in the air and created a ghostly dance of death. An ethereal haunting ballet. Softly, they descended upon the annihilated terrain, cloaking the ground in a thin, funereal layer of dust. The flakes cast a cloud over the planet's forlorn beauty. The Tesla plowed through the ash blizzard, windows obscured by billowing veils of obscurity, consumed by the eerie curtain of gray. In the rear seat, Charity slept, her delicate figure a painful reminder of the grueling hardships they faced. Atlas remained transfixed by the anomaly, poetically drifting back and forth. "Each day could be our last…"

Atlas watched and appreciated his daughter, her innocent sleep contrasted sharply with the gloomy reality they inhabited. He thought of the choice he made earlier of retreat. Doubts lingered in his mind. This current quest was a potential suicide mission. Starting over was an impossible gift that not even God themselves could deliver in a world enthralled in damnation. The man's contemplation delved deep into the corridors of his psyche as he pondered whether the lighthouse might offer them a second lease on life. Guided by the compass of his logical mind, he acknowledged the nature of his decision. A decision akin to the precarious balance of a coin wobbling on the edge where probability danced on a razor's edge. 50/50. Nothing could ever be entirely certain. The realm of particles themselves, adhering to Heisenberg's uncertainty principle, unfolded the unknown dance of chance, a reminder that even in the face of reason, the universe possessed an inclination for unpredictability. The man reached for the dwindling water and took a measured sip. The liquid offered only a momentary break from the unrelenting thirst that tormented him.

Atlas's steady fingers turned on the car radio. He waited patiently for a signal that would never come. Years ago, after the environmental collapse, every single radio signal went silent. The grid was lost, and blackouts reigned supreme worldwide. The Tesla's radio produced only silence that seemed to reverberate through the world's profound emptiness. "There's nobody out there anymore..."

Atlas's eyes met his own reflection in the rearview mirror. Ash flakes continued to rain down upon them as though Father Time was delivering a proclamation of deliverance. The man's spirit broke a long time ago. Outside of his wife and child, he never had a chance to experience joy. All Atlas knew was the challenges of existence. The man had read about happier times, but those were just stories of another era that he could never understand in the world of today.

Beyond the Tesla's windows, ancient skyscrapers towered—shattered monoliths reduced to a chaotic maze of fragmented ruins. These towering structures, now reduced to rubble, were once the marvels of a flourishing world. During the zenith of human civilization, innovation and ambition knew no bounds and resulted in the creation of those magnificent wonders. The era of capitalism fueled such endeavors, and it seemed that this prosperity would endure forever. Until the hellacious grip of the runaway greenhouse effect overwhelmed Earth's atmosphere and altered the course of everything.

Atlas remained focused on his daughter, her fragile presence a flickering beacon of hope in a world veiled in shadows. "In this dying world, my daughter is the sole lifeline that keeps me alive. Without her, I would have surrendered to the darkness long ago…" His gaze shifted, drawn inexorably to the pistol resting in his lap, a temptation of a quicker escape for them both. "In this world, the castaways and predators far outnumber the living. I'm afraid of the future that awaits my daughter when I'm no longer here to protect her from the evil souls that haunt Earth…"

Atlas tightened his grip on the steering wheel and approached a sprawling labyrinth of motionless vehicles. Rows upon rows of automobiles were unwittingly contributors to the environmental catastrophe, memorials to the infamous riddle that had shaped humanity's fate. The Industrial Revolution and the embrace of fossil fuels had been the lifeblood of progress, the evolution of human experience. Innovation, the foundation of human survival, had failed to bridge the gap between the green energy movement and the fossil fuel empires. The elusive invention that could have stopped the persistent march of the runaway greenhouse effect remained locked within the brains of human imagination. "Sometimes, in the darkest depths of my mind, I allow myself to entertain the notion of ending it all, for both of us. It would be the easier path, a release from the burden that weighs upon our existence…" The road ahead stretched into an unending horizon, a boundless expedition leading to possible impossibilities.

The Tesla found a destination in an abandoned parking lot. Everything was cocooned in an unending dance of gray ash, descending like a devilish tempest from the sky. The never-ending storm of unwelcoming particles divulged a sinister transformation. Ashes enhanced the world's complexion. In the land that once roared with fire, ice now held dominion. Day and night were starkly distinct companions. When the sun descended, a dramatic shift gripped the land, turning Earth into an ice world. Daylight was a temporary intermission from the unforgiving cold. In the middle of the frozen tundra, a cryptic enigma appeared, a *Vantablack complex* of impressive elegance. Its architecture defied the extreme weather conditions. In a desperate bid to survive the climate catastrophe, structures like these spread across the globe. They represented humanity's last-ditch effort to eke out an existence in a world plagued by a crumbling atmosphere. The Vantablack complex, a masterful creation, consumed light, and defiantly waged war against the glacial cold that descended in the dead of night. A monolithic figure in this frigid realm, a guardian for survival. These colossal structures used to be vibrant entertainment venues, designed to allow humans a brief escape outdoors in a world slowly succumbing to its downfall.

Atlas gently woke Charity from her deep sleep. Her eyes slowly flickered open as she emerged from the realm of dreams. In the daughter's dream, she soared through the sky, her vision spanned over the planet, as she surveyed the world from a vantage point only the dreamscape could offer. "Are we... shopping?"

Atlas, the eternal insomniac, was denied the gift of dreams. His voice carried sleepless nights. He murmured, "We need a shovel..."

Charity's eyes wandered beyond the Tesla's window, her aqua eyes beheld the God-forsaken cityscape. The ash flakes continued to reign down in a flurry, creating a magical painting of the apocalypse. Ashes upon ashes, it was a surreal phenomenon, one that even the most lucid dreams could not comprehend.

Inside the mall, a galleria of futuristic wonder permeated the air. Holographic Pi symbols twirled and shimmered— ghostly echoes of the advanced technology that animated this space. In the old world, Pi technology represented the pinnacle of artificial intelligence, a realm where humanity became immersed in a universal consciousness. In those days, words held little meaning. Humans transcended conventional communication and delved deep into their extraordinary cerebral capacities to birth thoughts and emotions—a cautionary tale of tragedy for language and human interaction within personal contact. Pi technology delved into the maze-like reality of neural-link systems and offered mobility and vision to those whose physical impairments or blindness had confined them. A multifaceted savior dependent on the eyes that beheld it. Within its innovative design, it wove connections between humans that transcended the wildest dreams of any other technology.

Behind the vacant storefronts, an abyss of darkness loomed. The faint, haunting glow of the Pi symbol—the only sole source of illumination—cast spooky shadows that danced like phantoms on the walls. Skeletal remains of former prosperous shops and boutiques stretched out in desolation. Rusted escalators, their mechanical souls long extinguished, lay twisted like fallen angels. The echo of footsteps on the cracked floor resonated through the immense halls, a ghostly reminder of the bustling consumerism that once reigned there. Flickering neon signs, their vibrant hues reduced to dim, sickly glows, offered cryptic messages. Atlas and Charity ventured deeper into the labyrinth as their footsteps stirred up clouds of dust, the particles dancing in the feeble glow of the Pi symbol. The mall felt its soul of capitalism silenced forever.

Atlas glanced at his atmospheric watch. Its digital display revealed the pollution levels: 5,779 ppm. The abstract nature of the problematic parts per million number remained a difficult concept that humanity, despite its collective endeavor, could never quite unite behind or fully grasp. It had an intriguing history; when the dinosaurs ruled the Earth, the number was believed to have reached a staggering 1,200 ppm. A time deprived of humans, this theory posited that the higher the number, the more serious the circumstances surrounding breathable air quality. The numbers glowed ominously and were direct evidence of the contamination that hung in the toxic air.

Charity remained fixated on the mysterious Pi logo. It called to her, an irresistible pull that tugged at her curiosity. She had read about the advanced artificial intelligence technology known as Pi, but never had she ventured into its realm. To her, Pi was a magician's trick, a digital Houdini crafting wonders out of the void. It embodied the mystique of creation from nothingness—a modern-day sorcery that promised to reveal its secrets only to those who dared to take the plunge into its puzzling depths. Charity became quite fascinated by science; she knew logical reasoning spoke the truth for nature. "We should have paid attention to the numbers. They were trying to warn us…" The world they had inherited was choked by its own vices and excesses. The atmosphere had become a harmful antagonist, a continual reminder of humanity's foolishness.

Despite the fatal gases that surrounded them, Atlas pressed forward, within this bleak reality. Forward became the only direction left. "Humans hate math…"

Charity continued to scrutinize the Pi symbol, her thoughts reflecting on its profound significance. The mall itself showcased the battle scars of shattered windows, discarded garments, and fractured technology. A dystopian creation of consumerism left behind remnants of capitalism. Atlas gestured towards the mall's upper level. They walked on an unpredictable ascent via a dilapidated escalator. Along the walls, they encountered a myriad of posters, one of which stood out, a depiction of a *blue embryo* nestled within a fallopian tube, accompanied by an evocative quote:

In the beginning there was water.

No water. No life.

A sheepish grin crept across the father's face. "Water was the cradle of life…" Charity's eyes lingered upon the poster momentarily before shifting towards a nearby *computer*. In the ancient world, these marvels of engineering held dominion over human existence. The computer, a creation of immense power and potential, promised efficiency and progress. However, as with all things in the complicated aspect of the human experience, it brought with it another paradox. The computer, while enhancing the efficiency of daily life, also scattered the focus and communication of humanity. Within the diversity of humans, it gave rise to a multitude of divergent opinions and perspectives. Knowledge became limitless, a boundless sea at the fingertips of all. A gateway to unending distractions, a double-edged sword of both enlightenment and escapism. In the old world, each user of the computer had a unique experience. Some harnessed its power for good and advanced knowledge. Others fell victim to its siren call and descended into the depths of detachment from reality. It became an invention that divided and polarized the world, showcasing the contradictory nature of human behavior.

In the ancient world these creations from engineers held immense power and control. The computer made life more efficient for humanity. It also invoked humans to become more unsure about their fellow species. For within the diversity of humans, the emergence of diverse thinking roamed rapidly when the computer was available. The computer released a unique aspect of human behavior: They had unlimited knowledge at their fingertips. They also had unlimited distractions. The computer was an invention that allowed fantasy and gave each user permission to craft their own unique experience. Some good, some bad, some ugly. It divided humanity and polarized the world of yesteryear. Charity was enamored, infatuated even, with the unique invention. She ran her gloved hand across its weathered frame in complete awe. Another piece of history that she read during her autodidactic pursuit of knowledge.

"Is that a computer?"

"Yes… It used to be our God…"

"How could a machine ever be considered a God?"

Atlas resumed his stride, prompting Charity to follow. The man knew about the archeological layers of history that absorbed the chronicles of humanity's fall from grace. The descent was triggered by the lure of computers. In his solitude, Atlas had become a scholar of sorts, well-acquainted with the unstoppable march of technology, symbolized by Moore's Law, the doubling of its computational power. He recognized the seductive promise of silicon and the siren call of an easier life that it whispered to humanity. He was no stranger to the darker side of this invention and the way computers fragmented society. It was a technology that had the power to fuel the fires of human rage until it left individuals isolated to choose machines as their closest friends instead of their fellow human beings. The man contemplated the enigmatic dance between human progress and the isolating grasp of machines.

"Long ago, computers held immense powers. They were the gateways to knowledge, the architects of innovation. People believed they could solve any problem, unlock the secrets of the universe…" Their journey through the decrepit mall continued, a crusade through the vestiges of a lost era.

Atlas and Charity moved through the darkness, gliding through obscurity. Their bodies cast shadows that glowed from the ethereal Pi symbol. They moved with a quiet vigilance, navigating the hardware store's depths as though they were hunted creatures. Their footsteps reverberated in the inky interior, every sound magnified in the tense atmosphere. Dust particles drifted gently down from the skylight, each tiny mote capturing the moonlight. The particles were wayward spirits of the night. Atlas, vigilant and armed with the shotgun, cast a watchful eye over their surroundings. He lowered the weapon slightly, but it remained ready for action. "Check the other side."

Charity nodded in silent agreement and ventured deeper into the labyrinth of pandemonium. Her search discovered nothing of value. Shelves lay barren, devoid of any useful supplies, and held insignificant items that were useless. Suddenly, her hands uncovered a *book*. Curiosity ignited a spark in her aqua eyes as she delicately traced the cover with her fingertips. The book displayed Earth in haunting infrared, a global canvas that vividly portrayed the devastating consequences of the runaway greenhouse effect. Determined, she carefully placed it into her weathered backpack.

Atlas ventured toward another aisle and scanned empty cases stripped of their potential potent contents. There were no knives, no guns, not even a hint of ammunition. A solitary *shovel* behind the depleted display caught his eye. "There you are…"

Just as he reached for the shovel, a sinister interruption shattered the standoff. Charity, held captive at knifepoint by a *frail man* concealed behind a gas mask that bore a malevolent *skull* symbol, commanded Atlas's full attention. The intruder carried a rusty oxygen tank, adding an ominous element to his frailty. The shovel released from Atlas's grip and fell to the ground. Without hesitation he instinctively raised his shotgun, its barrel trained on the intruder.

"What bring you to my home?" the frail man croaked, his voice no more than a gurgle.

"We didn't know," Atlas spoke his presence as resolute as the mountains. "Release my daughter, and we'll vanish."

The frail man's gaze lingered on Charity. "Good-looking girl." Charity stood frozen, her being shaken by the harrowing ordeal of the hostage attempt. The words she had read about such life-threatening moments felt inadequate to describe the visceral experience she was living through. The raw reality of the situation had left an indelible mark on her psyche, forever altering her perception of the world. The daughter, for so long shielded from the fear of death by her father's protective instincts, was now suddenly thrust into a chilling perspective she had never truly comprehended until this encounter. The reality of her mortality loomed and formed a dread upon her innocence.

The father remained firm in his stance, "You've got one minute to decide." Atlas recognized these men all too well, their ruthless survival instincts perfected by the unforgiving world they inhabited. In this apocalyptic landscape, it was the savages who thrived and demanded the cruelest of choices. The knife was dangerously close to Charity's throat; her body tensed with fear. Atlas inched forward, attempting to defuse the volatile situation. He understood where the most basic instincts of survival reigned supreme, he had to be vigilant. The frail man was a prime example of the ruthless castaways who had abandoned all vestiges of humanity. They lived by the lawlessness of survival, where compassion had no place, and the strongest thrived at the expense of the weak. It was a world stripped to its rawest, most primal form.

Charity pleaded desperately to her father. "Dad, help me."

Atlas remained alert during the standoff. Cool, calm, and collected. "Stay calm, sweetheart. He won't harm you if he values his life."

The frail man, a wretched figure, bristled with a deranged desperation. He was a man adrift in the chaos of a world gone mad, his sanity lost to the brutality of survival. Such men had forsaken all hope and lived only for the anarchy that had consumed their souls. They were nihilists in a world stripped of its meaning, where belief in any form of salvation had withered away like the dying embers of a forgotten fire. The frail man stared into the soul of Atlas. "Drop the gun! Or I'll slit your daughter's throat!"

Atlas slowly released his grip on the shotgun as the weapon fell onto the ground. The father raised his unarmed hands in a gesture of surrender. He understood that violence often birthed only more violence. Another approach was necessary in this delicate dance of strategy. "How can we make this work for you?"

The frail man reveled in his evil power play, his true intentions hidden behind the mask that obscured his face. Only the threatening skull emblem remained a window into his intentions. Death's shadow loomed over Atlas; the life of his daughter hung by a tenuous thread. The frail man's demands grew more insistent, pushing them to the brink of a decision with no clear way out. "Give me the water!"

From the depths of his trench coat, Atlas produced a bottle of *water*. He tossed it toward the frail man.

In the treacherous twilight of their encounter, the frail intruder leaned closer to Charity. His raspy voice, like the whisper of an enigma, carried secrets unknown. He murmured cryptic words into her ears, his intentions obscured in the blackness of night—only a ray of moonlight beamed upon them. Charity slowly scrambled to retrieve the water, the knife never wavering from her throat. "This was never a negotiation. Women are hard to come by these days. I'm going to borrow her." A chilling, remorseless cackle erupted from the intruder's parched lips, echoing through their confrontation. A sound devoid of humanity, an alarming call to madness. The creepy voice carried through the air, leaving a haunting imprint. The frail man was on a self-destructive mission. His hollow eyes revealed a complete indifference toward murder. In his twisted perspective, the events that were unfolding were nothing more than a morbid form of entertainment in the purposeless world he inhabited.

Atlas held firm, fully aware that the frail man was destined to end his daughter's life, regardless of the course of action he chose. Atlas remained unshaken by the dangerous situation; he was the only hope of saving Charity's life. "Give her back, otherwise I'm going to kill you."

The frail man, despite Atlas's comment, remained resolute in his position of power. He knew he held the upper hand in this confrontation and showed no signs of giving in. "Are you insane?" The frail man leaned close to Charity, his frightening whispers sending shivers down her spine. "What do you say, baby? We could have some fun." With cruel intent, the frail man tore off Charity's oxygen mask, causing her to gasp and struggle to retain her breath.

Charity dropped the water bottle. She coughed and grimaced as toxic fumes invaded her lungs, instantly suffocating her. A searing pain ignited instantly within the daughter, a fiery ache that clawed through her chest with every agonizing breath. The daughter, on the verge of losing consciousness, started to slip away. Death creeped closer, its cold embrace inching ever nearer. The father understood each fleeting second was critical in his desperate rescue attempt. The frail man laughed maniacally, reveling in the chaos until his eyes locked onto the rolling water bottle. In a swift and desperate motion, Atlas retrieved the concealed pistol from behind his back and fired. The bullet struck the frail man's face, killing him instantly.

Charity gasped for breath and fought with every ounce of her being for each precious breath. In her mind, she saw only darkness, an abyss that seemed to beckon her towards Father Time's eternal welcome, urging her to join it in the infinite expanse of eternity.

Atlas swiftly hurried to her side, quickly positioned his hands on her oxygen mask, and meticulously placed it back onto her face. "Put this back on." Charity hastily grasped the oxygen mask, her trembling hands fumbled to secure it in place. With a deep, shuddering breath, she felt the oxygen flood her lungs. The thin line between survival and death. She had narrowly escaped the clutches of mortality. Atlas quickly retrieved the water bottle and tucked it securely into his jacket as he scanned the area. His senses were sharpened; every sound was amplified in the silence. Danger lurked around every corner; where there was one threat, there were likely others.

In the distance, piercing screams shattered the stifling air, wrenching Atlas's focus back to the present. His eyes fixated on a group of *humans;* their gas masks branded with more creepy *skull* emblems. The figures carried menacing *chainsaws*. They moved with a savage grace, these marauders of the apocalypse. Fierce predators unleashed upon the world without a shred of humanity left within them.

Atlas, his instincts honed by years of survival, communicated wordlessly with Charity. His body language conveyed the urgency of their departure. Amid these ruthless hunters, their only chance was in escape. "Grab the shovel!" Charity grabbed the shovel and braced herself for the impending confrontation. Pandemonium reigned as the father and daughter raced through the labyrinthine aisles, exiting the hardware store.

The rhythm of gunshots echoed off the walls, each precise shot from Atlas's shotgun found its intended mark. One of the attackers was shot directly in the chest, collapsing to the ground. Panic washed over the chainsaw-wielding gang as they scattered, frantically seeking refuge among debris that littered the area. Driven by the will to live, Atlas and Charity surged toward the staircase, the deafening cacophony of chainsaws growing steadily louder behind them. Fear became their motivator; their breaths came in ragged gasps as their hearts hammered against the backdrop of madness. One of the chainsaw-wielding adversaries careened down the rail until Atlas's precise shot brought their reckless descent to an end. Adrenaline surged through their veins like a frenzied river. The father and daughter pressed forward with urgency. They had no choice but to keep moving, to keep running from the predators that pursued them.

In a sudden move Atlas whirled around, his shotgun roaring to life, as he sent a lethal bombardment of bullets that tore through the air. The attackers were compelled to seek cover again, their savage advance halted by the onslaught of gunfire. With desperation propelling them onward, the father and daughter raced closer to the escape promised by the exit. Their world had evolved into a maelstrom of brutality. Every stride they took served their unbreakable will to endure. They escaped the interior of the structure only to find themselves locked in another standoff with two *vagrants* wearing *anonymous masks.*

The vagrants were weighed down by weathered oxygen tanks that clung onto their backs. In this dystopian landscape, desperation drove humans to the brink. Vagrants, driven by the primal urge to survive, would stop at nothing to secure even a drop of water when it was available. Survival instincts reached a fever pitch, and they would materialize from underground, appearing wherever weary travelers roamed. Their souls scanned for vital supplies. In this unpredictable world, one couldn't afford to let their guard down for a second, as dehydrated wanderers lurked at every turn. They would be willing to go to any lengths to quench their thirst. The vagrants clutched the jugs of water tightly. It became the focal point of their encounter.

Atlas raised his shotgun and fired a warning shot that sent a thunderous echo through the tense, twilight atmosphere. "Put the water down! Now!"

Among the vagrants, a *woman* covered in dirt and filth, her anonymous mask marked by soot and dust. She remained resolute in the face of her circumstance. The woman appeared frail and malnourished, a scavenger doing whatever it took to hold onto life. The desperation within her drove her to the brink, and with a fierce determination, she declared, "We need this!"

A primitive primordial instinct kicked in for Atlas, who aimed his shotgun and pulled the trigger. He was the guardian of their water and would stop at nothing to protect it from intruders. The deafening roar of the shotgun was the harbinger of the dirty woman's demise. The water jug slipped from her lifeless grip.

During the heart-wrenching scene unfolding before him, a *young boy* covered in dirt and tears in his eyes charged toward Atlas and Charity. His innocence shattered by the brutal reality of witnessing his parent killed right in front of his eyes. "You killed my mother!" The young boy ran with vigilance, wrath spewing from his eyes. "Coward!"

As the boy drew near, Atlas noticed the bloodthirsty chainsaw gang inching closer, having exited the Vantablack structure. The crescendo of chainsaws was getting louder. A little louder. Even louder. Atlas, left with no other choice, fired another shotgun round, this time striking the dirty boy's leg. The boy crumpled in agony, his cries of pain echoed into the twilight.

Charity stared in disbelief, her young eyes experiencing the desperate act her father had been compelled to commit. "What are you doing?"

The father remained stern as time was running out. "Get in the car!"

Charity retreated to the safety of the Tesla as instructed, seeking refuge from the escalating chaos. Atlas approached the wounded dirty boy, his shotgun trained on the masked face of the suffering youngster. "Live or die?" Atlas stared down the barrel of the shotgun, as his eyes darted back and forth between the dirty boy and the maniacal chainsaw gang. The feeling of death crossed the boy's mind; he knew there was no escaping its undeniable clutches. Death had arrived, and he grappled with the options before him. Either way led to the end. The only question he could ask himself was which one would be the quickest. Option A: Choosing a bullet. Option B: Choosing the chainsaw. He whispered, "Die…"

Charity watched in silence, her soul in remorse from their actions. Atlas made a choice and pulled the trigger to deliver a merciful end to the boy's suffering. They both knew the seriousness of what they had done. When faced with the voice of reason in a waterless realm, death became the only option for thieves who sought after the most precious resource on the planet. After that dark moment, Atlas moved with purpose. He retrieved the gallon of water and hurried back to the Tesla with Charity inside waiting urgently. Atlas slid into the driver's seat, and as he did, the car assumed control, autonomously propelling itself forward into the unknown. They accelerated away from the Vantablack structure, leaving behind the pursuing chainsaw gang. The terrible noise of those cold-blooded machines slowly receded into the distance, while they fled the haunting horrors of the world, forging ahead in their quest for survival.

Charity looked out the back window. She captured the surreal scene of the chainsaw marauders descending upon the defenseless dirty boy with savage brutality. Consumed by hopelessness, the toll it imposed upon her spirit became unfathomable. Each moment of violence etched deeper into her psyche and forever made a lasting imprint. The daughter's aqua eyes continued to watch as ashes from the heavens poured down like tears from an eternal rain.

* * *

In a long-forgotten time, aerial vehicles and colossal rigs glided with grace above the superabundant ocean. These monstrosities labored 24 hours a day for years during the time of the drought. Their complex machinery relentlessly extracted seawater, drawing it up from the fathomless depths. Ships, with their cargo holding labored essential supplies, churned through the waves, their engines pumping heavy quantities of carbon dioxide into the already burdened atmosphere. Machines, like mechanical titans, labored tirelessly to pump ocean water into the atmosphere—their efforts to rejuvenate the ailing biosphere, a symphony of technological intervention. Human engineering persevered during this time. In contrast, the exponential extraction of water destroyed the global climate system. A chain reaction of factors, combined with the runaway greenhouse effect, transformed Earth. The enormous amounts of energy produced during this endeavor caused environmental and ecological disasters. The planet's equilibrium transformed, creating disruptions across the globe.

* * *

Emaciated *protestors* gathered outside the guarded *water plant*. Black oxygen, foggy and misty across the skies, persisted everywhere. A single breath could cause irreversible harm to anybody who dared to take a breath. Their gaunt faces were obscured either by the necessity of oxygen masks or the makeshift veils fashioned from tattered cloth. Desperation had etched its cruel mark onto each face. The humans were frail, clutching empty containers that were symbolic of their unquenchable thirst. Some found peace in prayer and sought refuge in their faith, while others recited scriptures, their voices echoing in dismay. The water plant used to be a place of abundance, until it became a forbidding fortress. Its gates were guarded by armed soldiers, their emotions hard to read as their faces were draped with oxygen masks. These soldiers were protectors of the peace, but now, in the face of the water scarcity, they had become the enforcers of survival. Their eyes, hidden behind tinted goggles, scanned the crowd with vigilance, ready to answer any sign of rebellion. They were all victims of a merciless fate, trapped in an unrelenting struggle for the most basic necessity of life. Water had become a commodity more precious than gold and a source of conflict in a world reshaped by the environmental collapse.

Protestors grabbed and pulled on the gates that guarded the prized *desalination* water tanks. Their collective union pulsated across the air with each shake, a poignant statement to the tenacity of the human spirit. Behind the fortress gates, armed soldiers had their weapons aimed for action. The protestors were overmatched by the soldiers.

In this totalitarian state, the game of desperation drove humanity into scary risks for the sake of their livelihood. The political system failed humanity. The system, in its internal decay, paid a somber homage to the greatness of the ancient Greek and Roman empires. Across history, it had remained a truth that any kingdom, no matter its power, was bound by the undefeated grip of time. Fated to crumble in the sands of its own ambition. Governments worldwide asserted total control over the lives of its citizens, in the vein of Hitler during the inhumane holocaust. In this dystopian reality, disagreement met with ruthless suppression. Individual freedoms had become a distant memory. The world plunged into a dark abyss where those in power reveled in their dominion.

Chants of "water is life" roared from the protestors. They continued their unwavering unification with nonstop defiant assaults upon the gates. A spectrum of human emotions danced across their faces: Anguish, hope, and defiance. The protestors understood that their existence was contingent upon the breach of the formidable gates. Tension escalated on both sides, until the thunderous arrival of *helicopters* descended from the polluted skyline. Ruthless accuracy was unleashed from a storm of bullets upon the helpless crowd, raining death upon the protestors. Bullets tore through the unarmed crowd and panic gripped their hearts as the protestors scrambled for retreat in a frantic bid for survival. A mass genocide of significant proportions occurred that day, forever changing the landscape of law and order during the environmental crisis. Evolution reigned supreme, along with the poetic motto, "Only the strongest will survive." The world had descended into a brutal arena where strength was the only regulation. Justice collapsed, buried beneath the rubble of a civilization that had crumbled under the weight of its own failures.

* * *

The Tesla rumbled forward, westward, along the deserted road, surrounded by a hushed hubris that felt as archaic as time itself. Time flowed like a slow river, carrying unspoken thoughts. Weariness etched into the hearts of Atlas and Charity. Murdering an unarmed woman and child was no easy choice for the father. The father harbored knowledge and knew that murder was a grave transgression against the sanctity of life. It was an act he deemed to be morally reprehensible and inherently immoral.

At last, the daughter shattered the oppressive stillness, her voice perplexed. "Why did you have to kill them?"

The father spoke the logical facts. "We're trying to survive… You know how rare water is these days… Life has become a treasure… Humans are determined to do whatever it takes to live… They'll fight for it until the end of time."

"You have to stop killing..."

"Why?"

"Because it's wrong! If there's any hope left for us, we have to stay good."

"We have to do whatever it takes to survive..."

"They didn't want to hurt us."

"Then they shouldn't have tried stealing from us..."

"Do you hate people?"

Atlas considered her question, his eyes locked on the measureless road. "I've learned to see the worst in people..."

Charity listened intently, learning the hard facts about her current species. "What happened to humanity?"

The father's wise eyes locked onto the daughter's innocent eyes. "The drought unleashed the evilest aspects of human nature. These times are full of desperation. Laws and moral codes hold no control anymore. What remains is only chaos."

Charity, who held redemption near her heart, remained optimistic. "But that doesn't define who we are... There must be a way to find the good in people."

Atlas, holding damnation near his being, remained pessimistic. "Those days are a distant memory."

"Are we going to turn into bad people?" Charity watched her father's emotional turmoil persist.

Atlas wrestled with the gravity of his choices, the moral dilemmas that carved their path through this wicked world. "We're protecting ourselves. It doesn't make us bad people."

"I don't want us to be like everybody else on this planet."

"Neither do I..."

Silence embraced them amidst the darkness, exposing them to an unknown future. Hope was as scarce as water. Their spirits were a flickering ember, a small flame of defiance against the encompassing night. They knew that the road would be treacherous and filled with uncertainties. The father and daughter understood the path of despair, a fate they could never accept. So, they pressed on—two souls bound by a fragile aspiration. They dared to believe that even in the bleakest of times, there remained a chance for salvation.

* * *

A bedroom glowed in the golden hues of sunlight, embracing Angelica as she occupied the edge of a bed. She cradled a *newborn girl,* the embodiment of innocence, in her loving arms. Angelica contemplated having a child during the apocalypse. She constantly was forced to decide which aspect made more sense in her reality. In her philosophy of life, she concluded that there were mysteries that would forever elude her understanding. She found peace in the simple act of being and savored each passing moment as if it were her last. She had the ability to find meaning no matter the dire circumstances. In the room's entrance, Atlas appeared in the doorway, his focus fixated upon the irreplaceable life enfolded within Angelica's arms, baby Charity. Uncontaminated purity in a world overthrown by evil. Angelica leaned closer, her lips gracing Charity's forehead with a tender kiss. A mother's unspoken love transcended space and time. "Never lose hope, Charity…"

* * *

Gray flakes drifted earthward in a mournful waltz. The ash continued to rain down at a blistering pace, a universal cremation that consumed all of humanity—past, present, and future—and reduced every soul to ashes. Charcoal flakes danced gracefully beneath the crimson glow of the moon.

These flakes were a haunting resemblance to the cataclysmic Permian extinction event millions of years ago when volcanoes erupted across the globe, heralding one of the planet's five mass extinctions. These flakes of death were reoccurring visitors during the apocalyptic Earth. At present, as the sun dipped below the horizon, the inferno world transformed into an ice world. Unyielding cold spread through the air, carried by punishing winds that blew through the forsaken landscape like vengeful spirits. Prophets of old had long debated the world's final fate, torn between the twin specters of fire and ice. In this bleak reality, both harbingers cloaked the planet like an inexorable curse, sealing its doom. Frozen tree stumps, like mummified remains, created a labyrinth of death. Where life once thrived, these vestiges had become collateral damage that succumbed to the apocalypse. Nature's haunting monuments inside a world forever changed.

Amidst this frozen wasteland stood a solitary *tent*. A durable shelter. Its structure, carefully insulated against the dangerous outside elements. It offered safety from the bone-chilling cold that raged outside, sturdy yet fragile, a pure judgment call from the Father. He placed his faith in probability and chance. He trusted that the tent would withstand the assault of the elements. Dust clouds swirled in a disordered dance around the makeshift camp. Any prospect of atonement was destined to submit, dissipating into nothingness.

Atlas pressed on; his movements were similar to a religious figure seeking guidance. His life hinged on the journey to the coast. The man wrestled with doubt, questioning the validity of his chosen strategy to save his daughter. He held onto the belief that in the face of challenges, the only path forward was to keep moving. This motto helped him hold onto a semblance of faith himself. Atlas came across an arid riverbed, his quest for water giving nothing more than acidic puddles. Each step through the dead forest was an exhausting task. His only companions were the shotgun clutched in his hands and the compass necklace that hung heavy around his neck. The Father, his mind adrift in the depths of existential contemplation, delved into his psyche. The man always had profound philosophical questions that haunted his soul. "Billions of years ago, Earth looked this way. We now find ourselves repeating the haunting footprints of history..." The shovel rested silently beside the flowing lava, the fiery inferno that broiled beneath the Earth's subterranean realm. "Underground rivers of molten fire flow. Water inches closer to the abyss of extinction..."

A vengeful mist led Atlas to a bleak clearing where *stacks* of *animal carcass skeletons* released toxic fumes into the polluted sky. This scale of death had spread across the planet. Animals were exterminated long before humanity's own struggles began as photosynthesis decreased. It altered the delicate balance of carbon dioxide systems and shifted the delicate composition of the atmosphere. The man spoke gravely. "Darwin's whispered truth echoes survival of the fittest. We have become the creators of our own destruction..."

The phantasmagorical fog submerged Atlas. In the murky depths of nothingness, all vision was lost, swallowed by the obscurity of smoke. It flowed and swirled, a cryptic force. Sparks of flames danced, a magical symmetry between the devilish and the angelic, creating a ballet of light and darkness. Through the blinding smoke and fire, emerged a rational voice. "Even Earth cannot survive the apocalypse..." The Earth's crust continued its release of gases, an unstoppable outgassing process that reshaped the turbulent atmosphere.

* * *

Angelica's compass necklace gleamed in the blazing sunlight. She found herself tangled in a struggle with a *wiry woman*. Amid their fight in the badlands, the oxygen masks and tanks of Angelica and the wiry woman became entangled.

A web of primal instincts allowed their brutal combat to be played out with savage intensity, culminating in a haunting conclusion. The wiry woman thrust a knife deep into Angelica's abdomen. An anguished gasp escaped Angelica's lips as her trembling hand clutched her wounded stomach.

Atlas spoke somberly about the tragedy. "My wife, was another statistic in the endless casualties for water…"

Abruptly, a gunshot tore through the draconian stillness. The bullet pierced the wiry woman's chest, and she crumpled lifeless atop Angelica. Both their existences were reduced to a trivial footnote in the cutthroat chronicles of this remorseless world. Smoke exhaled from the pistol as Atlas observed his wife's murder. His biggest regret in life was not saving his soulmate in time.

*　*　*

The tepee whipped and whirled in the violent environment and held no assurances. Its canvas walls strained against the intense winds. A small, concealed fire inside the tepee was reduced to minimal flames, its warmth an illusion in the cold of night. The compass necklace gently swayed in the fire. Atlas, his eyes heavy with exhaustion, watched that pendulum motion with an avid intensity. The muted glow of the embers created shadows upon the tepee's walls, as if the spirits of the land were converging upon Atlas. The night was nothing more than a black void that whispered secrets of loss and regret.

The welder's mask lay discarded in a corner of the tepee—a mask that protected the father from the evil world and concealed his emotions from enemies. Beads of sweat glistened on Atlas's furrowed brow. His psyche carried an endless war that was waged against his own demons.

Outside, the howling wind carried mournful cries, a haunting chorus that seemed to echo the ache in Atlas's heart. He had come to this forsaken place seeking a pause from the human predators that hunt them. He desired rest to absolve himself and his daughter, for he knew many more challenges were on their path. The sin of murder haunted the father's soul, a necessity in the twilight of humanity. He had never harbored the desire to extinguish a life, but in the end of days, he found himself shackled by a choiceless fate. As the compass swung, he couldn't help but wonder if he was a lost soul, adrift in a world where the boundaries between reality and dreams were blurred beyond recognition.

In the scarcely more-than-a-hole-in-the-earth, Charity stirred from uneasy sleep. The daughter awoke from a nightmare; the imagery of her father repeatedly committing the heinous act against the mother and boy seared into her mind. Charity saw her father, kneeling in silent contemplation, his eyes like two distant stars in the universe.

The father, soul on the edge of prayer but restrained by an unspoken composure, refrained from seeking help. His thoughts were noticeable, a heavy presence in the already cramped space.

With a deliberate and careful movement, Charity reached up and unfastened the leather straps of her mask, its surface caked with dust. Charity's face was etched with concern, her aqua eyes mourning a life that had known hardship from the beginning. Her father's eyes met hers. In a world where every breath was a rarity and never promised, it was through such moments of unspoken understanding that the bond between them grew stronger. They were managing the terror of navigating the deceptive world together. Both holding onto the fragments of humanity that remained within them. Even in the middle of chaos, their powerful relationship remained intact—a reminder that love, connection, and the enduring strength of family remained undefeated.

Atlas, his face a mosaic of weariness, lowered his hand and grabbed the pistol from the dusty earth. He extended it toward Charity, the weapon's warm metal shined faintly. "Here. Take it."

Her hesitation was apparent as fear clouded her eyes. "I don't want to use that." The daughter could never fathom the prospect of taking a life.

The father continued to explain the harsh truths of their current circumstances. "I don't want you to, either. But it's for your protection just in case I can't get to you in time."

Reluctantly, Charity accepted the pistol from her father's outstretched hand. She had never gripped a firearm until that very day. During her disquieting juncture, the daughter maintained a cool calmness as she clutched the pistol. Her aqua eyes traced the barrel's design, its form resembling a vital instrument for protection. She understood there was no turning back, no retreat from confronting the bad humans who crossed their path.

Atlas's body was exhausted from their confrontations; he felt the energy in his bones running dry. The man contemplated the realm of sleep, a peculiar but necessary state, and understood that within its mysterious embrace was the healing of the body, a vital act. The man was a fighter and refused to show weakness in front of his daughter. Atlas rested his back onto the dirt, his soul hardened by the grueling odyssey that stretched ahead. "The first time is always the hardest when you kill somebody..." Charity clutched the firearm, its deadly steel a dangerous reminder of the barbarous world. The man's weary eyes drifted to sleep, and within the labyrinthine confines of the dreamworld, he discovered joy and pain. Some dreams offered a comforting emotion, while others proved to be dark thoughts of the mind.

* * *

Inside the farmhouse, gentle muted sunlight sifted through a dusty window. In the kitchen, the delicate silhouette of Charity, who was only three years old, balanced precariously on her tiptoes by the sink. Her angelic face glowed with a pure, unburdened happiness, as she partook in a whimsical ceremony. Water swayed back and forth in the bucket, a fluid, divine motion, an everlasting verse. The daughter playfully splashed water onto her face, a delicate indulgence in a world deprived of luxuries.

The father, a man adapting stoicism, wordlessly advanced toward his daughter. His weathered fingers gently enveloped her tiny arm, and his face conveyed a complex mixture of disapproval and profound affection. Where each droplet of water was a thread of life itself, such youthful exuberance was rare. It was a unique gift to see an innocent smile during the end times. Charity's cherished excitement filled the room of endless possibilities and provided a scenario where life in theory could take a turn for the better in a multiverse of scenarios.

Atlas guided Charity's tiny hand towards the bucket, an allegory of their Spartan survival in the waterless world. Atlas dipped a modest portion of water from its depths. His hands tenderly scooped up a meager amount of water. The father gently splashed the elixir of life onto his daughter's face, an act that appeared inconsequential, a subtle droplet in the vast sea of their struggles. But in a realm where compassion had become an endangered species, it whispered volumes of devotion.

* * *

Within the derelict chapel, the sun's dying breath wheezed. Weathered walls beckoned for the arrival of a monster to burst through. Atlas was perched on the creaking pew, dressed in his armor of survival. He was once a man of faith until he witnessed the frailty of existence when a cruel twist of fate stole his wife away. He had forsaken the comforts of belief and opted instead for nihilism, recognizing it as the truth in life. In that bleak philosophy, he found the strength to fight in the endless apocalypse. The man knew there was no afterlife beyond the veil of reality. There remained a longing in his heart, a yearning for belief to rekindle miracles that seemed impossible to grasp. Atlas, weary from the weight of the world upon his shoulders, gazed into the vast expanse of the indifferent cosmos. He held a desperate desire to believe in some benevolent force guiding the chaos below. Yet, beneath the facade of hope, a cold truth gripped his soul—in the silent stretches of eternity, there existed no celestial hand to temper the undeniable truth of time. The heavens remained silent, indifferent witnesses to the ceaseless unraveling of a universe devoid of divine intervention. The man waited for the miraculous intervention that escaped him, like a phantom slipping through the cracks of his being. No magic descended from the heavens and his hope remained an unanswered prayer, lost in an indifferent world.

Around the dilapidated pews, a congregation of worn souls searched for faith. A collective spirit of confusion, an invisible cloud that enveloped them all. At the pulpit was a *fragile priest*, the living embodiment of their faith slowly disappearing. The skinny priest had a spotlight in a flicker of candlelight. His quivering voice wove a sermon as bleak as the world outside, each word a testament to the misery. Men, women, and children, their faces concealed by the embrace of oxygen masks, gathered in desperate communion. The believers prayed for a miracle in the deepening darkness.

The sermon carried on, each word a cry for dreams long buried. As the frail priest neared the conclusion, he closed the Bible to think. The sadness of the congregation was relative; their tears flowed freely but silently. Their cries muffled by the masks that secured them to life, a species on the verge of vanishing.

The frail priest turned to face the crucifix that watched over the altar. With a fearless decision, he reached into his cloak and produced a *revolver*. The cold steel met his temple, and with a single pull of the trigger, he killed the fragile thread that held his existence.

Atlas harbored no illusions. Every dawn seemed more unforgiving than the last; the concept of humanity determining its own destiny took on a rational view. It was the honest recognition devoid of mercy, where logic, perhaps, dictated the most pragmatic path forward. In the face of death, Atlas understood that the choice of each person's fate rested solely in their own hands. Suicide, a cruel and unspoken truth, remained the best-kept secret harbored by countless souls in the depths of their suffering.

The gunshot's deafening echo shattered the silence in the church, sending shockwaves through the souls of the stunned congregation, who experienced yet another loss. Faith, like so much else, had long since abandoned its throne. The concept of human sacrifice had evolved into a rite of passage. A way for humanity to sever its ties with the tyrannical planet.

* * *

With eyes open from his dreams, Atlas, his strength rekindled, lifted himself up from the rocks as though he were Lazarus emerging from the dead. In the quiet of the night, within the tepee, Atlas reached into his pocket and withdrew a stack of money. The pale bills, one after another, met their fiery fate in the crackling heart of the fire. Each bill that fell ignited and transformed into ashes. Flames performed their ghostly ballet. The shape-shifting shadows fell upon Atlas's worn face. "Our leaders possessed the means to make changes, to prioritize our planet and the generations unborn. Instead, they chose the path of denial, turning away from the warnings as if they were inconveniences."

Charity was nestled beside him, her eyes locked on the hypnotic dance of the flames. "Now we're paying the price for their ignorance," the daughter said candidly.

Charity hesitated, her fingers trembling as she held the pistol. With a determined blink, she aimed the firearm, discovering an unexpected steadiness in her grip. Atlas kneeled beside her, his weathered hands gently guiding hers. Together, they held the pistol, a warning symbol of their world, to the choices they were compelled to make in the face of fate. Atlas spoke boldly. "Scientists tried to warn us…" Charity scrutinized the pistol for markings, her young features etched with concentration. Atlas continued, "Our leaders turned a deaf ear to nature's wisdom."

With a heavy sigh, Atlas released his hold on the pistol, and Charity stared at it, her thoughts weighed by the gravity of their existence. "Everything feels so hopeless."

"We never give up…"

"Don't make promises you can't keep…"

Atlas reached out and took Charity's hands in his, his gaze unwavering as he peered into her eyes. "We'll find a way. We always have." The father understood the daunting trials that were waiting along the road. For the sake of his daughter, he was a believer; it wasn't the faith of God, but rather the stubborn denial of death. Where the spectrum of mortality existed, his belief was a defiant act of rebellion against the inevitable. Charity inhaled deeply, attempting to steady her nerves. The father noticed. "Close your eyes. I want to share a story with you."

Charity closed her eyes, giving in to the sound of her father's tales. In these moments, they embraced the sacred tradition of passing down knowledge through the art of storytelling. It was a practice as old as humanity itself, an oral tradition that predated the written word. The ancient Greek philosophers understood the power of spoken narratives and believed that through the spoken word, stories transcended ink and parchment. Spoken narratives were vessels for the wisdom of generations to travel across the ages. In the flickering firelight, their stories carried the weight of history, an enduring testament to the human spirit.

* * *

The Māgha Pūjā festival unfolded its pageantry. A multitude of Monks, their faces hidden behind oxygen masks, gathered at the temple grounds. Their voices mixed in enlightenment and harmony—an otherworldly chorus as they intoned age-old prayers and offered profound respect to the Buddha. Their devotion remained a sacred light amidst the void. Atlas began reflecting on legends of Earth's transformative philosophies, "Religion created sacred beliefs. It gave the human journey meaning."

Earth, an ancient witness to cataclysmic ballets, danced upon the precipice of annihilation with each passing age. The cycles of creation and obliteration etched themselves into the scarred face of the planet, always encountering the ebb and flow of cosmic indifference. This would always happen until the sun, a fading ember in the cosmic void cast its final shadows upon the world, forcing Earth to face its own demise, one day. A silent reckoning with the inevitability of dissolution in the universal crucible before the sun's fiery disintegration consumed even the echoes of its own existence. In the shadowed corridors of time, Earth trudged through epochs marked by the ceaseless rhythm of extinction, a macabre dance choreographed by forces unsympathetic to the fragile ballet of life. The bones of vanished civilizations lay entwined with the soil, departed ghosts to the extraterrestrial reckoning that awaited with patient inevitability. Until the final act unfolded, when the dying sun cast its supernova upon a world haunted by epochs of vanishing, Earth endured the pendulum of extinction, a stoic observer to the grand tragedy scripted in the celestial theater of its own departure.

Earth's core shook furiously as volcanoes awoke in fury, releasing molten rivers of lava. The heavens held onto tumultuous clouds of noxious gases—a terrifying spectacle and reminder of nature's unpredictable forces. Earth reigned supreme as humanity's God and was unswayed by prayers or offerings. Earth was a God whose will unfolded with no purpose. Billions of diatoms, a single-celled algae which played a significant role in oxygen production, drifted in the sea. Their job was to absorb carbon dioxide from the atmosphere. They were responsible for regulating Earth's oxygen balance. Now, the minuscule and insignificant cells meandered through the depths of the ocean's abyss—their existence a mere transient whisper into the vast aquatic ocean as they withered and ultimately died due to the uncontrollable amounts of heat. Atlas spoke candidly. "Science emerged from the depths of human curiosity and showed us the truth."

The smoke rose and blended seamlessly with the timeless grains of sand, conjuring a surreal image in the limitless Sahara Desert. A sight that defied the realm of the ordinary. A transient mirage of another world emerged from the heart of the arid wilderness. The dunes were whispers of eternity where nature painted its own enigmatic masterpiece. Atlas reflected, "Earth was a miracle to life." The boundless desert stretched out for infinity. An expanse adorned with the skeletal remnants of ages past, a haunted picture of fallen civilizations. The ghosts of history whispered their tales of rise and fall, a warning etched into the sands that had witnessed it all. The man remained settled in his tone. "Mother Nature unveiled her power, shaping the course of our destiny. Earth, not God, decided the fate of our civilization."

* * *

Back in their shelter, Charity's eyes resembled orbs of doubt. Atlas's eyes were locked onto the crackling flames. The man pondered on the profound narrative that wove together Religion, Science, and Earth. During the oscillation of fire, they found themselves entangled in contemplation, seeking meaning amidst the chaos that had become their world.

"I wish there was something else I could tell you."

"Why do we keep living when it all seems so... meaningless?"

"It's not our moment to cross paths with death."

"How can you be so sure?"

"You'll know when the time comes. Death has its way of finding you."

Charity absorbed her father's words with wisdom settling upon her young soul. The father recognized that, at this stage, his daughter possessed the resilience to accept the straightforward truth. Hard lessons were part of their journey, an education. Regardless of whether they emerged from it alive or dead. The father believed that comprehending all facts, even the abyss of questioning, was the only way to navigate the quest to the coast they embarked on.

The Tesla moved with elegance, gliding silently over the rise and fall of the Rainbow Mountains. Here, the forces of nature had etched their mark upon the land. Majestic peaks towered like ancient behemoths, their colossal stature forecasted deep-shadowed valleys over countless centuries. The panorama unfolded before them in breathtaking proportions. These mountains possessed a consciousness of their own. Each one proudly displayed its chromatic treasures. The rocks, sculpted by the passage of epochs, created an enchanting mosaic of colors. There were deep reds, engaged with burnt oranges, conjuring an ethereal warmth. Golden yellows brushed against the evergreen hues, fashioning a mixture of shades that dared to defy the limits of human imagination. The hand of time itself painted an ancient masterpiece that spoke of the earth's artistry. Even within this breathtaking view, humanity's transgressions revealed themselves. The former air, crisp and invigorating, ended due to the assault of an overabundance of carbon dioxide. Even the most magnificent of landscapes could not evade the consequences of mankind's undeniable undoing.

The Tesla pressed forward, its noiseless engineering guided it towards a panoramic view that slowly unveiled itself on the distant horizon, an *annihilated city*. Skyscrapers— former proud artifacts of another era, ancient monuments to human aspiration—laid destroyed and decimated. Their jagged remains rose like tombstones to the heavens. The city's architecture murmured ghostly echoes down the forsaken streets. The Tesla navigated and maneuvered its way through the urban expanse, showcasing the annihilating power of cataclysmic upheaval. Clusters of decimated buildings were reduced to skeletal remains, etched by the second law of thermodynamics, entropy. The foundation of chaos, a fundamental aspect of reality that's undefeated.

The road showcased countless scars of atomic storms, a chilling portrayal of humanity's destructive dance with nuclear war. During the aftermath of the climate apocalypse, desperation clawed at the hearts of humanity. The unthinkable was considered as a potential solution to stop the advance of the runaway greenhouse effect. Governments across the globe, in a difficult homage to history's horrors, embarked on a sinister path of destruction reminiscent of Hiroshima and Nagasaki. Major metropolitan cities, vibrant with life, became the epicenters of a chilling endeavor. The world's powers, haunted by the spectator of environmental collapse, resorted to measures that defied the essence of humanity itself. The echoes of atomic annihilation, a warning of the devastating potential of human conflict, became an eerie prelude to a desperate bid for survival in a world on the brink of cataclysm. In the darkest of hours, the moral compass of civilization shattered. A cataclysmic genocide lingered across the Annihilated City, a poignant reminder of the world's transformation into a cautionary tale.

Back in the Tesla, Atlas's eyes fixated on a blinking red light on the dashboard, a signal of significant trouble. An adrenaline rush ran through the daughter's body. "Something's wrong with the car, Dad."

The father knew the seriousness of the situation and remained emotionally calm. "We've got to get out of this city."

The Tesla malfunctioned and convulsed with sputters and shakes, compelling Atlas to execute an emergency stop. The electric vehicle grounded to a sudden halt. On the dashboard monitor was a chilling revelation: 51,008 ppm. The numbers indicated the dangerous state of the world's air in the current area. 51,008 parts per million of carbon dioxide, a disastrous calculation of Earth's poor condition. The balance between life and death was measured in those haunting digits. The concept of a middle ground had long since been swallowed by the tide of environmental decay. During the days when life still existed on Earth, the parts per million numbers were a source of controversy. Science and humanity stood at odds, two separate forces unable to find common ground. What should have been a pursuit of shared interest instead descended into a political battle where victory remained elusive. When the planet approached the brink of disaster, disagreements between science and humans became a reflection of the world's inability to unite in the face of doom. In this fractured landscape, the concept of a victor was lost to Mother Nature.

Atlas stared deadpan into Charity's eyes. "Put your mask on and stay inside."

Charity remained resilient and did not want to just watch. "I can help, Dad."

The father reassured his daughter; he saw fire in her eyes. "If you see any threats, shoot them." Atlas remained stoic as he secured his welder mask and stepped out of the Tesla. The man had no room for indecision. Time, a limited resource, propelled him forward. His vigilance assertive, he clutched his shotgun and methodically surveyed the Annihilated City that enveloped the Tesla. His eyes scanned the ground beneath the vehicle; he found no immediate cause for alarm. Atlas opened the panel, retrieved a replacement battery, and embarked on the meticulous task of swapping out the dead battery.

Suddenly, a disquieting sound pierced the silence. The echo announced an unexpected emergence of a *manhole cover*. From the murky depths, a figure emerged dressed in assembled lead and steel armor, an improvised suit of protection. An antique oxygen tank, and in his grip, a sword, the tools of a muscular *knight*. The knight, his form swollen and bulging like a titan from the myths of old, possessed a hulking, superheroic physique that dwarfed all who dared to stand in his shadow. The makeshift armor wrapped around him, a shield against the assault of the sun's powerful rays. The presence of another living soul, a phenomenon seldom encountered. The knight was stunned. "It's a rare sight to find another soul alive. Might we have a word?"

Bang! Atlas unleashed the shotgun's thunderous blast, splitting the sword apart. The blade clanged against the ground. The sword was no match for the shotgun, forcing the armored knight to toss the weapon. "No need for a conversation," Atlas declared, his words final. Charity, tugged at the door, capturing her father's attention. "Close the door!" he urged, his voice urgent. Defying her father's reprimand, Charity remained transfixed with the unique encounter. She kept the door open.

The knight continued his approach toward the Tesla. The knight pressed forward, his medieval armor imposing against the hostile backdrop. "Such a lovely young lady you have there," he remarked.

Atlas remained resolute. "Stop right there, or you're dead," he warned, the words hung in the air.

"Can you spare some water?" The knight's voice, muffled by his visor, carried a plea that cut through the dystopian world. "I promise, I'm not a bad guy," he added, his words a frail echo of humanity in a world where trust was scarce as water. The knight persisted in his march ahead. Atlas issued a stern response with another warning shot; the discharge of his firearm deflected off the knight's armor. The shotgun shell ricocheted off the impenetrable plating, a futile attempt against the impressive armor. The knight showed no hesitation, no pause, while he continued his advance, driven by a purpose that seemed to breathe new life into his soul.

Sporadic gunfire erupted from a crumbling skyscraper. From the depths of the shadows, an unseen *sniper* fired a deadly shot. The crack of the rifle cut through their world as it attempted to find its mark on the father and daughter. A sudden storm of bullets peppered the Tesla. Atlas and Charity found themselves entangled by another ambush. "Charity, get out!" the father's anguished cry cut through the chaos. Charity emerged from the battered Tesla, a vestige adorned with bullet holes. Above them, the skyscraper towered. A rapid number of bullets cascaded from the skyscraper like a deadly avalanche, sweeping through the Annihilated City with ferocity. The father remained both creator and destroyer for his daughter, knowing that the slightest hesitation would thrust her into inescapable danger. "Find cover!"

"What about the water?" The daughter's voice quivered as she huddled behind the damaged Tesla. "I'll get it! Just go!" The father's voice remained by her side, against the encroaching threat. Atlas emerged from his defense position behind the bullet-riddled Tesla. He fired his shotgun, punctuating the air as he fired a volley of cover shots. It was a desperate attempt to allow Charity the precious seconds she required to make a daring dash for safety.

The knight's determined advance caught the attention of the sniper concealed within the crumbling building; their sinister body language gave the sniper a thumbs up. Down on the ground, the storm of bullets continued to intensify. The gunfight between Atlas and the sniper was a persistent bombardment of violence.

Charity, a coiled spring of nervous energy, waited for the elusive right moment, that brief sliver of opportunity, and when it finally presented itself, she burst forth, a blur of determination. Charity spotted a decrepit *warehouse* and ran straight for it. She was in the open and vulnerable. The daughter had no choice but to find her way from the ruckus. Closer, step by agonizing step, she ventured, each careful movement burdened in jeopardy of being shot. And then, with a final, daring push, she arrived, hurling herself behind a decimated concrete structure. She found a momentary break from the bullets that seemed determined to hunt her down.

The knight seized Atlas, forcibly throwing him to the ground, causing the water jug to scatter. With brute force, the knight pinned Atlas to the earth, wrenching away his welder mask. The knight tightened his grip around Atlas's throat and strangled him, knocking the welder mask off. Atlas spotted Charity sprinting back toward him. The chaotic maelstrom continued raining down upon them. The daughter moved with a desperate urgency, narrowly evading the barrage of bullets. "Stay back!" Atlas tenaciously held his breath, demonstrating superhuman resilience against the toxic fumes, refusing to succumb. Caught in limbo between the unseen sniper's deadly aim and the fight of her father, Charity found herself entangled in an agonizing dilemma, trapped and unable to come to her father's aid, her helplessness pressing down upon her like a vice.

An ominous *acid rain cloud* loomed menacingly above; its venom cast a fearful veil. The acid rain represented the tears of a dying world, bearing a similarity to the fatal weather on Venus. A fury mirrored the respective planets.

Venus wept acidic tears from its violent atmosphere and the same anomaly gripped the Earth, unshackling its wrath in the form of a corrosive rain, a tribute to the unraveling of the world's equilibrium.

The cloud discharged its lethal payload while corrosive raindrops descended upon the blighted terrain, *hissing* and *sizzling* upon impact.

The knight's anguished cries filled the air as the *sulfuric acid* droplets voraciously consumed his helmet. His imposing armor became a bizarre spectacle of devastation. The knight struggled for breath in the noxious air under the stranglehold of carbon dioxide that filled his lungs. The knight's harrowing scream of agony tore through the air. Aware of the plummeting sulfuric acid, Charity swiftly found cover underneath the warehouse and narrowly missed the sniper bullets that dangerously zipped by her. Atlas employed the knight's body as an impromptu shield against acid rain, narrowly evading the dangerous droplets. The knight was no longer mortal.

Atlas gathered his composure, reclaimed his welder mask, and secured it in place. The sulfuric acid continued its relentless descent. A droplet struck Atlas's shoulder, searing his flesh. Smoke spiraled upward from his charred skin, yet he remained steadfast. Charity continued to back away from the acid rain and moved underneath the protection of the warehouse.

Atlas progressed toward the Tesla, where the sulfuric acid droplets waged a war of corrosion against the vehicle. Desperately dodging the lethal rain, Atlas retrieved the water jug and oxygen tank, leaving the suffering knight behind. Death by acid was a fate fit for the pages of fairy tales where the darkest imaginings could find their chilling narrative. Earth had evolved into this fairy tale.

Without warning, a deluge of *bullets*, fired by the sniper, peppered Atlas. The bullets struck his bulletproof vest, but

Atlas remained uninjured and persisted. Atlas accelerated his pace and sprinted away from the bedlam. An *explosion* occurred leaving the Tesla consumed by flames as it disintegrated into a fiery blaze.

In the heart of the deteriorated warehouse, Atlas's vigilant eyes swept the area as he remained shielded from the encroaching sector of evil that the rain produced. The haunting hiss of sulfuric acid droplets formed an unending chorus, relentless in its methodical assault on the frail remnants of the decaying warehouse. The corroded walls offered little support against the acid rain. "Charity!?" Atlas's voice rang out, carrying his fear as he kept searching for his daughter.

Emerging from the rubble and debris, Charity materialized, her presence filtered through the fractured ruins. Atlas examined his daughter, his hands searching for any telltale signs of harm. To his relief, she had no visible wounds. "Don't try to save me." Atlas implored. "Promise me you won't put yourself in danger."

"We've always taken care of each other," Charity insisted.

"Your life matters," Atlas emphasized. "It doesn't matter what happens to me. You must stay alive."

The tone of Charity's voice escalated, resonating with a fierce resolve. "I won't abandon you. We're stronger together."

"I have to make sure you have a chance at the future."

"What future? The world is dead!"

Beyond their brittle haven, the echo of acid rain became noticeably closer, and the sound rose in volume. The rain hammered the concrete structure. Searing droplets of the corrosive rain oozed through the fissured ceiling. A game of chance forced the father and daughter into a delicate dance of avoiding the dangerous rain. Vigilant efforts were made to evade the deadly droplets. Atlas and Charity moved meticulously through the decaying shelter. There was never a moment of rest for the weary, any instant could bring a harmful encounter with acid. The father and daughter found safety in a corner and hunkered down while they waited for the murderous downpour to stop.

"You can count on me to take care of myself."

"That's all I ask…"

Atlas and Charity shared a profound exchange, their eyes tracing the remains of the ravaged Tesla. Their former vessel of salvation was in the process of disintegrating. Acid rain had taken its toll, causing the car's framework to melt back into the earth, succumbing to the unstoppable forces of nature.

The father and daughter traversed a graveyard of forsaken *railroad trains*, colossal relics left to decay. Some trains were glued to the tracks, while others had surrendered to gravity and rested upon their sides. The ionizing iron tracks stretched onward and vanished into the horizon. Atlas concealed the water jug within his jacket, cradling its important contents, guarding their sacred gift from the ravages of their reality. He gave Charity the last remaining oxygen tank.

"What about your oxygen tank?"

"I'll make it last."

Charity skillfully replaced her oxygen tank, a task she had mastered. The daughter surveyed the train car graveyard and contemplated its past significance. Long ago, it had been humanity's vital heartbeat for the transportation of goods, a network that crisscrossed the nation and thrived. Now, it had dissipated to a blip on the radar of recollection, abandoned to a bleak crypt. This mode of transportation used to pulse with life until it was reduced to a tombstone of forgotten days. She whispered softly to her father, "The entire world faded away."

No longer did the rhythmic clatter of wheels against rails resonate through the land. The Industrial Revolution, a story of the ages, was buried beneath the dust. Machines and factories, which had ushered in an era of progress and innovation, had long since fallen silent, their mechanical hearts transformed by the fragile atmosphere. These echoes of industry became mementos of the world that once was. *Delivery tankers* were littered throughout the train yard. These hollow giants, guardians of commerce in a planet reduced to ashes, were parallel to tales of a time when their cargo was substantial.

Atlas approached a timeworn railroad train, his every movement deliberate while he released the latch. Shotgun in hand, he stepped back, his eyes penetrating the darkness of the interior. The heavy door slid open, revealing a horrifying sight: *Skeletons* spilled forth from the train cart, an avalanche of ancient, departed bodies that cascaded upon the father and daughter, their ghostly presence emblematic of the apocalyptic world that had taken control. The skeletons poured out on Atlas and Charity, an overwhelming flood of bones upon bones, an unrelenting tide that threatened to bury them in the shadows of death.

Atlas pushed away the skeletons, granting him and his daughter deliverance from this eerie tomb. From the plethora of bones, Charity emerged, her soul shaken to its core by the surreal and phantasmagorical reality of death. An intimate encounter with the departed, a visceral reminder of what was waiting on the other side. Mortality extended its bony grasp and seized the daughter's emotions, shaking the core of her soul with a reminder of life's fragility.

"We're going to die out here!"

"Quiet. People might be listening!"

"I don't care! We have guns! We'll kill you if you try attacking us!"

The daughter's scream pierced the God-forsaken heavens, an anguished cry that tore through the silence, revealing her frustration to any Godlike presence she desired to believe in. Fear had long ceased to be a companion, for she had surrendered herself to the madness of the waterless world, where the boundaries between hope and despair blurred into a fractured mosaic of purgatory.

"Everything will be fine."

"You're lying!"

"Once we reach the coast, it'll be like it used to be."

"Who gave you the right to choose for me!?"

"I'm your father. You do what I tell you to do."

Charity pressed the pistol against her temple. The daughter confronted the stark reality of her own mortality, her life now suspended precariously in her trembling hands. In this moment of profound desperation, the choice of her life was in her hands. It offered a resolution, an opportunity for divine salvation that held within it the power to bring an end to her suffering. The daughter had endured to her breaking point throughout their odyssey into the heart of this dominion. "What if I pull this trigger!?"

The father approached his daughter, his footsteps echoed softly. All-encompassing silence wrapped itself around them. No other souls remained; only the father and daughter remained. Uncertainty clung to the edges of his consciousness, a haunting ghost that danced on the boundaries of his thoughts. A chill ran down the core of his being, a reminder of the fragility of life. Here, the whims of chance and the unstable dance of chaos could determine the conclusion of their shared journey. The father couldn't help but wonder if this would indeed be their last living moment together.

"Charity, please don't. Give me the gun."

"Why? It can end so easily."

"Just put down the gun."

"Make the pain stop."

"Maybe tomorrow will be better. You can't leave."

The daughter's aqua eyes fixated on the water jug, a transient vessel of life in a world constantly veering toward emptiness. In her eyes, water was a fairy-tale creation; God put it there. Her faith stayed the course, recognizing water as the true sustainer of life.

"What happens when we run out of water?"

"We'll find more."

"How? With a shovel? Are we going to dig and hope for a miracle?"

"I promised your mother we would never give up."

"Mom's dead. She doesn't know what's happening."

"Do you know the meaning of your name?"

"That meaning is a ghost."

"Hope… Your mother and I knew the world was changing, but we held onto hope when you were brought into it."

The words of hope etched themselves into Charity's psyche. Slowly, she lowered the pistol from her temple. Each word from her father resonated deeply within her, a glimmer of fragile embers holding out in the cold darkness of their world. "Why?"

"Because your mother believed that one day, things would return to normal."

"Look what happened to her."

"It's not your time to die. Not today."

Atlas gently laid his hands on the pistol, easing the weapon from his daughter's trembling grasp. Charity slumped to the ground, and Atlas descended to his knees beside her. The dying world around them was an observing silent spectator. If the planet possessed eyes, it cast a watchful gaze upon the unfolding drama, cognizant of the struggle playing out upon its stage. Their connection transcended the nightmarish realm where time itself had lost its meaning. Time had come to a standstill, frozen in eternity, simply watching and acknowledging the enduring strength of the human spirit.

"I didn't ask for this life."

"None of us did…"

The father and daughter embraced, shielding themselves from the clutches of their dystopian world. Life and death, inseparable companions, walked hand in hand. The love shared between the father and daughter remained a supreme force that propelled them forward. A remarkable connection that resisted the obsessive pursuit of Father Time, who shadowed every step.

It is during our darkest moments that we must focus to see the light.
Aristotle

When there is harmony between the mind, heart and resolution then nothing is impossible.
Holy Vedas

CHAOS

Only when the last tree has died and the last river been poisoned and the last fish been caught will we realize we cannot eat money.
Cree Proverb

* * *

In the boundless realm of the cosmos, an eternal dance unfolded. Satellites twirled against the infinite darkness. Their choreography enhanced the limitless void with a graceful masterpiece. During the cosmic symphony, an abrupt anomaly emerged. The gravitational field, once a constant, underwent a transformation. Its altered state disrupted the satellites from their celestial waltz, and they succumbed to the endless pull of gravity, beginning their fateful descent towards the awaiting planet below. Through Earth's atmosphere they plummeted like fallen angels expelled from the heavens. Fiery trails marked their descent. The atmosphere ignited with each satellite's entry, birthing a series of cosmic explosions that punctuated the night sky.

* * *

In the barren backyard of the farmhouse, Atlas held Angelica close, her lively complexion drained of vitality. A cruel blade, an evil omen of their misfortune, protruded from her abdomen. Atlas's unsteady hand hovered over the weapon. He paused, concerned, as Angelica's whispered plea reached his ears. "Just leave it there..." The man understood that this would be the final chapter for his wife, her wound a fatal blow in a world where healthcare systems had crumbled long ago. Atlas tenderly brushed his fingers against Angelica's pale cheek, a futile attempt to ease her fear.

Beyond the farmhouse, the world offered no help. "Help us!" Atlas's voice echoed into the void, but they received silence in return. They were alone with no one to come to their rescue.

Angelica grabbed Atlas's hand, her hushed plea etched with an urgency that transcended words. Her dying eyes held a haunting awareness. Angelica understood that this was to be her final moment on Earth. Death hovered, a patient entity that encircled her being. Death, a profound enigma since the inception of matter, appeared to possess an inherent longing to order and chaos. In the ultimate reckoning, it seemed that reality itself harbored a yearning for destruction. Its substantial aura drew near, poised to claim her last breath. "Promise me something," she said, her voice grew softer as she wheezed into her oxygen mask.

"Anything…" Atlas replied as he tried to stay strong, awaiting her impending departure.

Angelica spoke a key phrase that would last forever in Atlas's psyche, "Keep our daughter safe…"

Tears streamed down Atlas's face, his devotion to his wife's dying wish clearly etched into the depths of his soul. He understood that the harshness of their existence would win. The man vowed to carry out his promise to his wife, a commitment that would endure until his final day on Earth.

Angelica's eyes shifted beyond Atlas's shoulder, and she saw their young daughter, Charity, just eight years old, standing in the background. She knew that this would be her final moment with her daughter, the inescapable grasp of death coming to a conclusion. With a weak smile, she whispered, "Hi, sweetie…" In this serene, haunting moment of fading life, the mother and daughter locked eyes. A woman's love for her child is a relationship unlike any other, a bond forged in the crucible of maternal devotion. For Charity, innocence was washed away by the wave of reality, and the approaching end. "I'm going to rest for a while. Your father will take care of you." Charity, overwhelmed by the gravity of the moment, turned to her father for reassurance.

Atlas held his emotions in check and prepared himself to speak his last words. As he leaned in, his voice spoke of the promise. "I'll protect her with everything I have…"

Angelica's grip on Atlas's hand grew weaker. She gifted Charity one final smile, a last expression of love. "Never lose hope…"

With a serene final breath, Angelica's soul quietly departed. Atlas held his lifeless wife close. Charity wrapped her small arms around her father, finding comfort in his presence. In spirit, the father, daughter, and mother remained united, cruelly separated by the unpredictable twists of destiny.

* * *

The train compartment was nothing more than a chamber of shadows in the middle of the night. Atlas's silhouette was distorted by a ragged sack draped over his head—a crude defense from the toxic air. His oxygen apparatus labored in a world choked with poison. With each rasping inhalation, Atlas fought to inhale oxygen. These precious breaths were no respiration; they were a harsh reminder to the will to endure, to persist against the cruelty of a world hellbent on crushing the human spirit. Atlas sat defiant in the face of adversity. His aura battled death. The man raised the water jug to his parched lips, the water trickling down his throat, a brief victory from the plague of thirst.

Charity remained asleep, undisturbed in her dreamworld. Her pureness continued to feel the repercussions by the hollow-hearted quest they wandered.

Atlas adjusted his welder's mask, obscuring his battle-worn face from view. Behind that steel barrier, his eyes settled upon an oxygen tank, its diminishing contents a constant aide-mémoire of their desperate situation. Atlas understood the journey of finding more oxygen was another problem that quickly approached. The currency of life had become oxygen, an elemental fuel for the dance of evolution, nurturing the emergence of complex life. Since its emergence during the Great Oxygenation Event, oxygen had traversed a transformative path and culminated into a carbon dioxide dominated planet. Earth had become empty from the life-giving breath that once defined its landscapes. Their world was an hourglass with the grains of air slipping away. Time, a cutthroat taskmaster, remained the man's inspiration. Rest, a luxury beyond his reach. Sleep, a leisurely indulgence, was a wistful dream. Every waking heartbeat was a miracle that could only continue if they won the day against the odds. Atlas knew they were locked in a race against time to find oxygen and water, where the weary dared not pause. Even a moment of rest could spell the end of their lives.

A book laid nearby, "*Our Angry Earth*," written by Isaac Asimov and Frederik Pohl. The cover depicted an inferno world—a planet aflame with fury—symbolic of nature's wrath, and a scientific curiosity of a time long since swallowed by the environmental collapse. "We were voices adrift in a sea of noise," Atlas muttered to himself, his words quiet. "Our words were lost in the past, carried away by the arrow of time." He traced his fingers over the book's faded pages. The pages held the wisdom of scientific investigation, now faded like the memories of a forgotten world. "Understanding," he continued, "slipped through our grasp like sand in an hourglass. Slipping away, second by second, until it was gone, leaving us to wander this waterless world, seeking answers we may never find." Atlas contemplated his thoughts, feeling history pressing upon him, a world's wisdom reduced to a whisper in the wilderness of their existence.

Atlas's grip tightened around the pistol, an intoxicating contemplation threatened to plunge him into the abyss of suicide. The steel of the weapon found its place against his own skull. The man thought long and hard about ending his life and his daughter's life in that moment. "We journey down a path by those who came before, joining the haunting legacy of Earth's history…"

In the distance, gunfire echoed through the Annihilated City. A violent crescendo punctuated by anguished cries that cut through the air like a knife. Chaos submerged them like crashing waves on a coast, threatening to consume all. The man understood that there was nothing beyond this life. The concept of an afterlife, a place of serenity, held no opinion over his thoughts. In his brutal reality, he pondered why one would choose to prematurely extinguish their life. Contemplating the void that awaited beyond, he found reason in the notion that, given there was nothing waiting for them on the other side, it adhered to be wiser to keep moving forward into the unknown. It was better to face the uncertainties and the turmoil of the world they knew than to speed up the inevitable with a desperate escape.

He held on to the belief that the struggle, the journey itself, held a purpose, even if that purpose remained elusive. To face the unknown, to witness the never-ending danger, remained a cruel gift of existence, even when faced with the certainty of oblivion. With a heavy sigh, Atlas lowered the pistol. His eyes locked onto the compass necklace cradled in his palm. Its delicate needle a symbol of the direction they must persevere, no matter the cost. The man drifted into a dream, his mind navigating the labyrinthine corridors of memory, retracing the blueprint of how the past unraveled into their present and uncertain future.

* * *

Within the dreamworld, an ageless structure, the ancient Mayan temple. Time's passion etched deep into every weathered stone. The Earth had grown weary of its own consciousness. The cloak of dust and grime draped over the temple's timeworn surface, hiding secrets that have long since passed. Tornadoes churned and twisted, darkening the heavens. Nature could care less about the world, as vengeful spirits of the atmosphere were unleashed. They were but a manifestation of a cosmic turmoil, indifferent to the struggles of those who walked this difficult land. In their waltz, they danced, mocking humanity. A mournful ballet, a memento of the world's descent into chaos. The stones, cut with purpose and precision, crumbled and decayed away, showcasing the decline of a civilization that lost its way.

Atlas spoke, his voice the timbre of wisdom honed through countless eons. "The ancients respected this world, recognizing its sacredness. Human progress altered the course of history."

The thriving Amazon rainforest had transformed into the depths of hell, a searing and desolate inferno. The mighty jungle had withered into a forsaken realm. All that remained was the Amazon Tall Tower Observatory, a lone guard in the desolation where the lush canopy of the Amazon basin used to thrive. It was now a dystopian wasteland. The air, formerly filled with the harmonious symphony of life, had fallen strangely silent. The vibrant chorus of birdsong and the distant murmur of unseen creatures had vanished. The observatory, a place of scientific inquiry and discovery, now became a monolith in the void. Its towering structure represented human achievement but carried the wounds of neglect. Shattered windows and rusted beams spoke of the decay and abandonment that had befallen the world. A beacon of knowledge and exploration had succumbed to the irreversible changes brought upon the planet. The winds whispered through the dying drylands and the shadows deepened in the fading light and served as a grave epitaph.

"The trees," Atlas spoke softly, his voice carrying sadness, "once guardians and the lungs of our planet, have become tragic casualties of our ambition."

God's country was erased. The *Redwoods* had been reduced to skeletons. The former majestic forest that possessed their towering glory was a memory of a world undone. The dead forest felt like purgatory from which no escape presented itself. Its twisted and gnarled trees warped into grotesque contortions. Their branches clawed at the sky, reaching out in a futile plea for redemption that would never come. In all directions, inhospitable wilderness sprawled, reduced to ashes—a reflection of the price humanity had paid for its mistakes.

Atlas spoke in a voice tinged with regret, "Every part of Earth's ecosystem was connected, each piece vital to our survival. Until our arrogance disregarded this delicate balance, sealing our own species' fate." His words carried the truth, echoing through the requiem for a paradise forever lost. The world became a shadow of its former self. Mother Nature crumbled, forever altered by the hand of self-destruction.

* * *

Atlas relentlessly exerted his muscular frame in the labor of feeding the voracious engine with coal. Beads of sweat carved rivulets through the well-worn grooves etched deep into his weathered brow.

Charity stirred from her sleep. She opened her eyes, her vision a murky haze of disorientation. For her, the world had become an indistinct blur, a shapeless and hazy experience. The protective mask, which had covered her eyes, had slipped away during her uneasy rest. "Dad," she called out, her voice a murmur in the presence of the machinery, "I can't see!" Panic gripped her like a vice, her hands flailing in the disorienting fog. She struggled to make sense of the world, her voice trembling with fear as she cried out, "Everything is blurry! What's happening to me!?" The daughter's mind compared her blindness to navigating an endless, ink-black sea. Every motion forward felt like a leap into the unknown. Her world was defined by the touch and sound that surrounded her.

Atlas's response was swift, a dance of practiced urgency. His weathered hands moved with a surgeon's precision, delving into his backpack. From its depths, he extracted a *syringe* and a vial of precious medical fluid. The father's touch remained steady, his nerves calm. With meticulous care, he set to work, preparing the needle with the skill of a seasoned practitioner. He extracted the vital remedy.

"Relax, sweetie! I'm going to fix you."

"Dad, where are you?!"

"Right here in front of you!"

"I'm blind!"

Atlas, with a tenderness that contrasted his rugged exterior, guided Charity forward. His hands, though they trembled ever so slightly, carried her with utmost care as he drew near. In a firm voice, he implored her, "Keep your eyes open!"

Charity forced her eyes open, wider than she believed possible. She braced herself, enduring the excruciating discomfort that came with it. Atlas administered the eye-saving treatment, one delicate injection after another, a unique operation of significant stakes.

After the emergency procedure had run its course, Atlas strapped Charity's mask back over her eyes, shielding her from the toxic environment. She blinked repeatedly, gradually emerging from the murky abyss of her blindness. A profound sense of relief washed over her, like a cleansing tide. She realized her vision had been restored. The daughter was beyond grateful and embraced her father with the strongest hug she'd ever given him—both bound by their life-altering shared ordeal.

"Thank you... What did you give me?"

"Stem cells."

Stem cells, in the domain of medicine, had paved the way for numerous groundbreaking advancements. It helped to repair organs, restore eyesight, and orchestrate regeneration in ways that seemed like the stuff of dreams. Atlas offered a silent nod, gesturing his weathered gloved hand towards a nearby jug of water. "Take a sip," he said, his voice a low reassurance.

Following her father's advice, Charity positioned her head under the sack, mirroring his earlier use of the oxygen apparatus. She took a refreshing drink, the cool water provided a victory. With a hint of concern, she questioned, "Are you sure about the coast?"

Atlas continued shoveling coal into the roaring furnace. The friction of coal against coal sparked a testament to the combustion of fossil fuels. The air, of old pure and untouched, had become overtaken from the Industrial Revolution—a tribute to the magnitude of emissions that had engulfed the world in darkness.

"Trust me. There's something waiting for us there."

"Water?

"A second chance."

"You seem so sure of everything. Out here, every moment could be our last."

"We keep moving, no matter what."

Charity nodded, her thirst partially quenched, Atlas set aside the shovel and made his way to the open doorway of the train. Her aqua eyes followed him, acknowledging his commitment. The father's mind drifted into the depths of contemplation. Hope and chance, elusive companions in this dystopian world, were the convictions that kindled his soul. Atlas stepped out of the train compartment, his boots landed softly on the parched earth. The man's eyes ascended to the heavens, where an eerie vortex of inferno patterns swirled, casting an otherworldly aura.

An *artificial intelligence jet*, its dark surface devouring light, streaked across the sky, booming straight for the Annihilated City. Charity's aqua eyes widened in awe as she watched the jet approach. Its presence in the polluted, dreamlike skies resembled a transient vision from another realm. The ominous weapon it carried purely designed for the sole purpose of creating destruction upon the leftovers of civilization. A deafening roar wallowed, immersing the Annihilated City. The weapon of mass destruction released its devastating cargo, an *atomic bomb*. It plummeted from the heavens, its descent marked by a silent grace, untethering unfathomable devastation. *Kaboom!* A blinding luminescence fractured the dark sky, emitting a radiance of enormous proportions. The world had continued to regress, time traveling backward to the darkest days of World War II. Atomic bomb explosions haunted the collective psyche of the globe. The soul of the world had been decimated. Atomic bombs represented a dark chapter. Misguided hopes held on to the belief that it could thin the human ranks and alter the trajectory of the climate catastrophe, simply by eliminating humanity, no longer allowing their appetite for energy and fossil fuels to exist.

Atlas watched the genocidal event unfold. The entire world had become a powder keg, armed to the teeth with nuclear warheads capable of creating a deadly mechanism of population control. The atmosphere *quaked* with thunderous shockwaves. An *apocalyptic explosion*. Charity watched a monstrous *mushroom cloud* unfurl on the distant horizon. The shockwave from the detonation was a beastly force, creating a deafening sonic boom that rippled through the air. It sent violent tremors that coursed through the train's steel frame. A colossal *dust cloud* of swirling particles moved in the direction of the train. It engulfed all in its path, a creeping sense of dread covered everything it touched.

Charity's eyes remained fixed on the evil event beyond the train's dusty windows. The world was submerged in demolition. Atlas returned to the train cart. "Time to go!"

"What's happening!?"

"They're killing survivors!"

"Why!?"

"They think it'll save the world!"

"Can it!?"

"No. Hold on tight!"

Charity gripped the rail, her fingers holding onto the metal as the compounds within the train, the burning coal, roared with unbridled ferocity, discharging its fiery power. Atlas yanked down on the lever, locking the train into full throttle. It hurtled forward, an iron behemoth driven by the goal of absolute survival.

The train's wheels grinded against the rusted tracks, their agonizing screech carved through the barren wasteland like a day of the dead march. Each passing moment surged the locomotive forward, its form gradually devoured by the thick, choking haze that overwhelmed everything in its path.

Atlas and Charity wrestled with the insanity of the aftereffects from the dust storm. The train quivered and lurched like a wounded creature, its massive frame at the doorstep of the whims of nature. Within this disorienting turbulence, the father and daughter fought to retain their foothold. A ferocious battle against the forces of nature attempted to cast them adrift.

Charity lost her balance and was violently torn from her father, the dust storm showing no kindness in its brutal separation. Atlas's strong hand reached out, his fingers closed around Charity's smaller, trembling one. The father's hand closed around his daughter's with a fierce grip, holding her close and refusing to let go. Their stronghold remained

119

unwavering, an anchor against the ferocious onslaught of the storm's fury.

The atomic blast defied the laws of nature, warping the fabric of reality. Gravity gave in to the magnitude of energy, its rules were rewritten. The jet, a fallen angel in this theater, its wings, powerless, all energy systems deactivated. The detonation set off a chain reaction that unleashed electromagnetic pulse functionalities, cascading through the electronic web of the jet. This effect cast the old world into the dark ages of technology. A profound *nosedive*, the jet's descent an unruly symphony of disarray. The aircraft hurtled earthward, its trajectory marred by a vengeful Mother Nature. The jet vanished into a speck in the storm, encountering forces far greater than itself. The jet lost its battle against the Earth, vanishing into the singularity of the storm.

The train plowed through the heart of the storm. It defied logic and pushed forward, each grinding revolution of its wheels created distance between itself and the Annihilated City. The thunderous roar of the engine grew louder, and the dust storm was gradually left behind. Heroic transcendence from the ancient vehicle of long ago allowed the father and daughter to avoid death.

Atlas and Charity stood at the window, their eyes locked onto the fallout of the atomic bomb's devastating impact. The father and daughter shared a silent understanding. There were no words capable of conveying the depths of the apocalypse. They were mere survivors in a world that had veered off its course.

* * *

The fragile globe continued its precarious wobble on its axis. The blast cast a diabolical glow across the planet's scarred surface. The world experienced countless extinction-level events over the course of eons throughout cosmic history. The atomic bomb explosion was but one in a series of unfortunate events during the saga of loss. From the vantage point of outer space, the bombing appeared as nothing more than a minuscule forest fire in the grand scheme of planetary turmoil. In comparison, the depletion of the oceans presented a far more vivid colossal catastrophe. The soul of the world seemed to weep. In the cold void of space, Earth remained suspended, a witness to its own undoing.

* * *

Charity stared at the purgatory sky where the gray ash flakes continued to descend. Atlas kept his attention locked onto the infinite train tracks that stretched ahead. Charity broke the silence. "Dad, have you ever wondered what it would feel like to experience rain?"

Atlas responded, his voice heavy with nostalgia, "All the time. Rain was a precious gift in the past."

In her childhood, one of Charity's most cherished memories was the moments spent with her mother. They shared stories of the old world when rain was plentiful, a divine creation from God, as her mother had described it. "Mom used to tell me that God would watch over us when it was raining."

Atlas embraced nature, valuing its timeless wisdom over the uncertain terrain of faith. The father watched the hellish sky, his weathered expression etched with pain. In the past, one of the main conflicts he had with Angelica revolved around the belief in a higher power that could fill the void of meaning. His nihilistic thinking had birthed atheism, a philosophy that held truth in these trying days. Atlas always told Angelica that he would present logical truths to their daughter as they encountered life experiences. He believed in allowing Charity to find her own path, but his convictions were firmly grounded in reason, especially in a world that did not guarantee tomorrow. "There's no afterlife waiting for us, those are ancient stories." The father's words carried conviction. All he yearned for was to let the unvarnished truth speak to his daughter.

Charity found herself contemplating the concept of death. Ghosts of mortality were thieves of immortality, stealing life within every waking soul in existence. From the experiences of their journey, she had wrestled hard with this notion. The daughter continued to hold a deep belief in the triumph of good over evil. "I've accepted dying with you," she quietly confessed.

Atlas thought long and hard about his daughter's beliefs in the context of their circumstances. The father understood that Charity was being pushed to her emotional and physical limits. Atlas reassured her, "You're not going to die." It was a promise he intended to keep, a desire to his Herculean spirit that had carried them this far.

The daughter understood that her father was attempting to ease her subconscious fear of mortality. She held onto her philosophy with life, devoted in her belief system. Charity's words carried a bit of wisdom as she spoke, "Yes, I am… and it's okay, because at least I lived a little bit. I would rather choose to have lived, even on this dying planet, over never having had the chance to live at all."

The father found himself captivated by his daughter's touching words. In her innocence, she had uncovered a profound understanding that left him in awe.

Charity suddenly noticed something outside the window. "Dad, look!"

Their eyes remained transfixed on a colossal and impassable *wall barrier*, an insurmountable obstacle that blocked the entire train track. Atlas clenched the lever and pulled it back with extreme force, striving to stop the advancement of the train. The piercing sound of metal scraping against metal screeched throughout the compartment. Their efforts to resist the crash were useless against the unstoppable momentum of the runaway train. Atlas's muscles strained while he tried to stop the train. It remained unstoppable to his superhuman strength.

Sparks flared as rusted train tracks etched onto the weathered wheels of the train. The shrill, distressing screech tore through the terra firma terrain. In a devastating sound, the brakes finally shattered their tracks to the train and plummeted to the earth.

Atlas clutched Charity's trembling hand; their fingers locked in a desperate union. "We have to jump!" he declared.

Charity locked eyes with her father, and in that shared look of understanding, she inhaled a sense of bravery, a reservoir of fortitude. "Okay, Dad," she whispered. Atlas nodded stoically. The mournful howl of the wind swallowed them whole. The locomotive's thunderous advance surged toward their cataclysm. The train inched closer to the wall barrier.

Atlas grabbed Charity and they leaped from the speeding train. They were suspended in the air, defying gravity's grip. Time unraveled, the world around them decelerating to a crawl as they descended, their bodies twisting and contorting in the deafening wind. Atlas and Charity hurtled through the air, their bodies specks in the world. Every heartbeat became an eternity, every breath an echo of doom. *Thud!* Atlas and Charity collided with the rocky ground. Their bodies tumbled and rolled, absorbing the brutal impact.

The train, a behemoth of steel and thunder, careened headlong towards the wall barrier as though destiny had ordained the collision. Its iron wheels screamed in protest, sparks cascading like fiery tears in the night. With an ear-splitting roar that seemed to fracture the heavens, the collision unfolded. The earth trembled beneath the force as the train's titanic momentum met the immovable wall. Metal groaned and twisted, a devastating impact that tore the train apart.

Atlas, his body feeling the searing pain of the fall, summoned reserves of strength as Charity rolled off him. In that fateful descent, the father's sacrifice served as a shield, absorbing the brutal impact from their leap of faith. Together, they rose from the dust, battered and bruised. They surveyed the wreckage of the train, both their lives barely spared from the unpredictable hand of fate.

Colossal *shadows* emerged, casting a fearful presence. A ruthless gang of predators closed their distance around their helpless prey. Silhouettes of military rifles, their metal gleaming in the inferno of sunlight, were trained with deadly accuracy upon the father and daughter. They raised their hands in an act of surrender, keenly aware of the gravity of their dreadful situation.

From the obscure shadows, a gathering of heavily armed figures emerged, their identities veiled beneath ominous military masks. An aura of enigma remained with their every step. Dressed like soldiers from an untold future, they were a legion of evil humans, united by their nefarious designs, their collective intent etched into the bedrock of their sinister game. The father and daughter found themselves outnumbered and overpowered.

The bodies of the *enslaved humans* showed scars of filth and emaciation. This city of the dead had long lost its chance at life, its landscape had become echoes of the ancient Middle East during the biblical times of slavery when the Dead Sea Scrolls emerged. Among the rubble, whispers of the past lingered like condemned souls. Homo sapiens, their necks and ankles bounded in chains, moved with a heavy, resigned step. Oppression had shattered their spirits.

Slavery, an insidious thread woven deep into the DNA of human existence, had endured since the first humans emerged from Africa. Through the eons, the backdrop had shifted, but the fundamental cruelty remained unchanged. It was the dance of the strong overtaking and controlling the weak, a manifestation of Darwinism in its rawest form. Even within the heart of the apocalypse, the grip of slavery maintained its supremacy.

A colossal crater stood on the road ahead, left by the impact of an asteroid. Under the iron grip of this tyrannical regime, humanity withered away, and freedom extinguished. Within the crater, an homage to the ancient Mayan Empire and countless other civilizations past, present, and future, that had carried out mass injustice without guilt. Countless decapitated bodies were littered throughout the crater. The phantasmagorical scene was the timeless darkness that resided within humanity. An ungodly force that transcended the ages and cultures stained the pages of history with unspeakable horror.

Heavily armored soldiers expressing dictatorship authority dominated the prisoners. They were an army of death without limitations to the wrath they could commit. Within their possession, they captured the father and daughter's single water jug, a taunting gesture to their dominance. These soldiers of the apocalypse carried a sinister reputation. They were enforcers of high, net worth individuals whose sole purpose was the extermination of unfortunate humans they captured, using their blood for hydration. This group had its roots in a brutal past, and their history was steeped in genocides committed against their own kingship. Their actions drew comparisons back to the darkest days of the ancient world when murder had been an everyday commodity for survival.

Atlas and Charity, their bodies trapped by the savage weight of the chains, trudged in unison with their fellow captives. The intense sun exacerbated the already excruciating conditions. "Dad, who are these people?" Charity finally broke the silence.

"The 1 percent. The rich with no regard for human rights," Atlas whispered, his voice heavy with resignation. "We have to find a way out of here; they're going to kill us." Atlas scanned their heavily guarded surroundings, a sense of hopelessness sinking into his bones. The odds of escape appeared impossible, an intense darkness closing in.

Anguished cries tore through the air, humans screaming at the heavens with all their might. Desperate pleas were carried on the wind, their urgency only to be abruptly silenced. One by one, the voices of humanity ended, replaced by the sickening, oozing sound of dripping—the darkness of evil immersed the God-forsaken world. Atlas spotted a grotesque *blood reservoir*. There, buckets filled with blood and gristle were poured by the soldiers, an unsettling brutality.

"What is that?" Charity asked, her voice trembling.

"Blood," Atlas replied, his words carrying the magnitude of truth. "They use it for hydration." Where water had become a long-forgotten dream, blood flowed as the vital currency of hydration, a substitute in the drylands.

Nearby, a military *Cybertruck* was idle, a formidable behemoth of bulletproof steel and glass, its angular, cyberpunk design a testament to the fusion of technology and brute force. Soldiers loaded barrels of blood into its bed. The line of captives inched forward, moving closer to their fate with death. Amidst the madness, the drifter from earlier, the one who wore a plague doctor mask, made a desperate bid for freedom. The soldiers instantly opened fire, their bullets extinguished his life without hesitation. The *executioner* materialized, a Grim Reaper aura, wielding a machete. With swiftness, the drifter's head was severed from his body, a terrifying event that sent shockwaves of fear through the watching captives. The soldiers, their faces hidden behind oxygen masks of cruelty, discarded the lifeless torso, treating it as a routine act of disposal. His lifeless form was ferociously discarded into the gaping jaws of the crater, swallowed by the void. The crater yawned wide and deep, its metaphorical resemblance similar to Jack's descent into the subterranean world beneath the beanstalk. An apprehensive pit that seemed to lead beyond the heart of darkness.

Atlas and Charity were gathered forward by a soldier, their inescapable fate drew nearer with each step. Fear consumed Charity, her small form hinged desperately to her father. "Don't let me die, Dad," Charity's voice trembled, her terror visible. She was unprepared to meet her end on that fateful day.

Before Atlas could utter a word, a soldier aggressively swooped Charity away from his sturdy grip, sending her crashing to the earth. Atlas moved with frantic urgency, his every attempt to reach her prevented by the hands of their captors. They stood as powerless prisoners, confronting the distressing certainty of their beheading. Charity looked at her father, her aqua eyes glistening with tears, while she braced herself for what seemed to be her end. A chill ran down the daughter's spine. She begged in her psyche for reassurance in the face of her potential death. Charity stared at the executioner's macabre theater. Her eyes pierced the executioner's menacing veil, revealing the crater—a pit of skeletons and lifeless bodies similar to rituals of ancient civilizations that performed self-sacrifices.

The executioner, a cruel puppeteer of fate, brandished his machete with vindictive joy, relishing the lethal authority it granted him. He reveled in tormenting his victims, engaging in a cruel psychological intimidation of 'eeny, meeny, miny, moe'. It was a chance moment when the executioner's machete would fall upon Charity, sealing her fate in the game of life and death. The soldiers dragged her before the executioner. He keeled down to stroke her concealed cheek, savoring the twisted thrill of his grisly craft. "Such a pretty face," he sneered, his voice filled with barbarism. "Perhaps I'll keep it as a trophy, may it savor the sweetest." The daughter couldn't help but think about the dreams she had cherished, knowing they would never come true.

"Kill me first!" Atlas's voice emerged from the depths of his soul.

The executioner, a master of maliciousness, cast a dismissive glance at Atlas. He expressed a chilling sense of control, the manifestation of a predatory force descending upon the helpless daughter. His actions, guided by an evil instinct, solidified his role as the venomous predator. "You'll have to wait your turn, Dad," the executioner spoke vehemently. He reveled in the torment he was about to inflict.

With an eccentric dance, the executioner taunted Atlas. He pretended to swing his blade at Charity's delicate neck repeatedly, a violent pantomime of psychological distress. Atlas remained bound by the overpowering grip of the soldiers; he could only watch in helpless anguish as the taunting performance unfolded before him. Trapped within the confines of the soldiers' restraints, Atlas knew there was nothing he could do to change Charity's fate. The father wanted to say final words that could offer some sense of hope. "Close your eyes, Charity," he said, his voice a frail shield against the encroaching darkness. "Think of your mother!"

Charity, trembling with fear, obeyed her father's command, squeezing her eyes shut as tears flowed down her cheeks. Terrified of the unknown, the daughter prayed silently to herself. The executioner, poised for the final fatal blow, raised the machete, his intentions evident, finally ready to decapitate the daughter.

In an instant, an unexpected eruption of gunfire pierced the stifling tension like a thunderclap. The executioner and soldiers were diverted by this sudden intrusion from the surprising ambush. Seizing the sudden opportunity, Atlas leaped forward with a surge of power, violently smashing the back of his head into the soldier restraining him. He broke free from their grasp and lunged at the executioner with ferocity. Atlas and the executioner tumbled backward, their bodies descending into the abyss of the crater. Charity watched the miraculous attempt by her father to save her life. The daughter made her own defiant choice. She skillfully evaded a gunshot aimed in her direction, then hurled herself into the crater, following her father into the depths of wickedness.

The trio tumbled down the crater, their descent marked by an unearthly journey over lifeless, headless bodies. Their fall felt never-ending as they tumbled down the steep decline, gaining speed with each passing moment. Charity found herself amidst a gruesome pile of bodies, a disturbing mosaic of skeletons intertwined with the freshly deceased. The enormous crater had swallowed them whole; they were entangled in the lifeless pit. Legacy of genocides were necessary evils that would never vanish from the face of Earth.

Atlas, still bound by chains, summoned the deepest reserves of his strength. He lunged for the executioner's throat, his fingers clawing at the air to stop the violent intentions of their tormentor. But the executioner, a formidable adversary, used his powerful legs to kick Atlas away, breaking his grip with a brutal efficiency that left them locked in a lethal dance of hand-to-hand combat.

The sky transformed into an apocalyptic destruction, lit by surreal explosions that painted the heavens. The sound of war echoed throughout the atmosphere, punctuated by bullets and deadly hisses of missiles—a chaotic intermix of warfare that resembled the history of all wars that had come before.

The executioner launched a powerful punch, his aim directed at Atlas's welder mask. Atlas blocked the blow with his forearm, absorbing the impact. In a swift countermove, he retaliated by delivering a brutal headbutt to the executioner, momentarily disorienting him. Atlas clasped his hands into a makeshift hammer, bringing it down with tremendous force upon the executioner's head, further dazing his enemy. Gunshots whizzed into the crater, ripping into the labyrinthine maze. Atlas dove behind a makeshift barricade of bodies, narrowly evading the deadly hail of bullets. Charity found safety amidst the grotesque pile of headless corpses, her small form hidden from the lethal crossfire.

Atlas's sharp eyes discovered a femur bone within arm's reach; he seized it for a weapon. The executioner shook off the blow from Atlas, retrieved his machete, and charged at Atlas, set on revenge. The two locked in a brutal and primal clash, the makeshift bone weapon against the machete. Neither combatant held back in their savage quest for dominance. Atlas and the executioner became two primal fighters, their desires for survival burning like a wildfire within the surreal environment. The executioner swung the machete wildly, a savage beast resembling that of an ancient caveman, slicing through the bone in Atlas's hands and gaining a momentary upper hand. He prepared for a final, fatal blow.

Atlas stumbled over a skeleton and tumbled to the ground. The man lay defenseless on the dirt, a vulnerable target for the executioner who showed no mercy in his brutal assault. Before the savage man could act, a single gunshot shattered the tension within the crater.

The bullet found its mark with chilling accuracy, piercing the executioner's visor, and extinguishing his life. He fell, defeated, an unexpected shift in the cruel tides of fortune. Atlas turned to find Charity, her demeanor cool and calm, complete control in her decision. She held the pistol that had delivered death's final verdict. The daughter thought to herself about taking a human life. Survival instincts, she realized, were a peculiar thing. Regardless of the consequences, she found an unsettling peace in her mind with the fact that she had taken her first life. Nothing would ever compel her to sit back and watch. She was now fearless by nature, her spirit had evolved.

Atlas seized the executioner's machete, holding it with a firm grip as the battle raged on above them. Out of nowhere, a couple of soldiers met their end, their deceased bodies tumbling into the crater. Mayhem consumed everything and everyone all at once. The father and daughter found themselves entangled in the heart of the warzone. With a powerful swing of the machete, Atlas shattered the chains that bound Charity, liberating her from their oppressive grip. Her eyes, filled with grit, met his. "Are you okay?" Atlas spoke gently, his voice a soothing anchor during the war.

Charity's eyes remained hypnotically fixed on the fallen executioner. The echo of her gunshot lingered in the air, a chilling reminder of the irreversible act she had just committed. Time stretched into an endless abyss as she embraced her actions. Within her psyche, there was neither regret nor remorse. Instead, a stoic acceptance settled in her mind. Charity's survival instincts had carried her through the dark decision of murder. Her young eyes, once innocent, had transformed into windows that peered unflinchingly into a world engulfed by violence. The harsh reality of their current existence had forced her to confront the darkness lurking within herself. Unable to find words to articulate the emotions swirling within her, Charity remained frozen in place. Her hands clenched the pistol, a graphic contrast to the warmth of her father's presence. She felt the weight of the world pressing on her shoulders, a burden no human should ever be forced to endure. The daughter knew there could be no turning back. During that moment of reflection, she found a spark of determination that would guide her through the evil that infected the globe.

"You had no choice," Atlas spoke calmly, his voice soothing in the aftermath of her ordeal.

"I'm fine, Dad," Charity replied candidly. She handed the pistol back to Atlas, signifying the shift in roles.

"Stay behind me," the father instructed, his voice a reflection of his protective instincts that guided him. Together, the father and daughter embarked on their hazardous ascent toward the crater's gaping opening, an arena of death.

Soldiers were in a face-off against Rebels, their motivations and allegiances obscured by the thick fog of war. Blood, the ultimate currency of survival, had become the coveted prize. A Soldier and a Rebel engaged in a struggle, their violent entanglement culminating in a fierce clash that sent them hurtling into the blood reservoir. The crimson fluid enveloped them both.

Atlas and Charity, two souls adrift in a world gone mad, navigated the terrain with caution. Their eyes, vigilant, scanned the battlefield, desperately seeking any scent of safety. The Cybertruck surged forward in a turbulent sea of violence and called them like a distant oasis. Emerging from the maddening chaos, a soldier, consumed by a thirst for victory, charged toward Atlas and Charity. However, fate, as cruel and capricious as ever, had other sinister plans in store. A hidden land mine, a silent arbiter of death, chose that fateful moment to unleash its deadly wrath, ending the soldier's advance in a deafening *eruption*. Atlas pivoted to Charity, his voice cutting through the chaos, *"Watch your step!"* Charity acknowledged her father's warning with a resounding nod.

The Cybertruck appeared untouched by the carnage that surrounded it and provided an opportunity for escape in a world where such chances were scarcer than mercy. The battlefield continued to showcase supreme mayhem. Out of nowhere, a colossal construction *dump truck* filled with

Rebels emerged, a juggernaut of death plowing through the soldiers with ruthless indifference. It crushed all in its path and was an unstoppable force. The tribe of rebels was comprised of the labor masses who used to be the backbone of the world. The rebels wore the attire of the working class: Rustic, weathered clothing. Strapped to their backs were oxygen tanks and masks. Most resembled ancient divers. Their conflict was a mere microcosm of the inner wars that raged in certain territories, all for resources. Blood wars had become a global phenomenon, a conflict that spread across the world, leaving no corner untouched by its savagery.

Atlas and Charity found cover behind a boulder, narrowly avoiding an encounter with the rampaging dump truck. Their lives, like countless others, were pawns in the game of survival. The boulder served as a shield, deflecting the barrage of bullets that ricocheted off its ancient textured surface.

Atlas's eyes fell upon a discarded grenade launcher abandoned in the dirt. He seized it with a sense of urgency. "Move," Atlas commanded, and Charity obeyed without hesitation. Together, they moved in the direction of the Cybertruck as the war raged around them, consuming everything in its path. Atlas aimed and fired the grenade launcher at the dump truck, a Goliath that must be defeated. Explosions ruptured the air, each grenade finding its mark against the massive vehicle with a thunderous roar. The world trembled as the dump truck lost control. Flames erupted and swiftly consumed the behemoth as it hurtled into the crater—its destructive power silenced in a fiery spectacle that illuminated the desolation like a shooting star in the night sky.

The grenade launcher, emptied of its deadly payload, was unceremoniously cast aside by the father. Atlas and Charity, their eyes locked onto the Cybertruck, pressed forward with even more tenacity. Each step brought them closer to the promise of escape, an oasis in the desert war.

The conflict intensified. Bullets continued to rain down with ferocity, their stinging impact echoing in the air. Atlas and Charity, edging ever closer to their goal, found refuge behind a cluster of rugged rocks, avoiding enemy fire. The war showed no signs of letting up and threatened to kill the father and daughter at any moment. Time seemed to stretch and warp as they caught their breath. With a mutual nod, they continued their pursuit, bodies propelled by the will to live. Each stride, each graceful evasion, brought them one step closer to the salvation promised by the Cybertruck. Bullets, those messengers of death, were nonstop. Atlas and Charity remained unafraid, their athletic nature impressive amongst the turmoil.

In a final surge of energy, they reached the Cybertruck, their hands grasping at the door handles. With a collective heave, they yanked the doors open, their bodies tumbling into the haven of safety. With a sudden lunge, a soldier leaped into the Cybertruck, grappling with Atlas, but the father's impressive strength prevailed as he overpowered the intruder and forcefully tossed him out of the vehicle. The doors slammed shut behind them, a barrier against the pandemonium that raged outside. Atlas swiftly ignited the dormant military vehicle. The engine roared to life as they accelerated away from the battleground of bloodshed, leaving the horrors of war behind in their rearview mirror.

A forsaken desert highway stretched into infinity, an open road where elements had eroded the concrete into cracks and decay. The Cybertruck roared down the deteriorating path; behind them, a fleet of military vehicles gave chase. Their pursuit was a hunting pack driven by the insatiable desire for the cargo of blood the Cybertruck harbored.

A blaring, frantic *beeping* disrupted the already tense atmosphere. Charity's wide aqua eyes darted around the confined interior, seeking the source of the urgent alarm. "What is that!?" Charity's voice trembled.

"Our oxygen tanks! We're running out of air!" Atlas spoke with urgency, the realization of their dwindling oxygen tanks unfolded.

Their adrenaline peaked. Charity's gaze fell upon the backseat, where their shovel was in a corner. Frantically, the daughter crawled into the back bed, her hands quickly searching for any reserve tanks.

The military vehicles, dark avatars of a tyrannical regime, gained ground. Each ping of bullets ricocheted off the back door of the Cybertruck, its surface encased in a bulletproof coating. The vehicle's protective shell held against the assault. Inside, the atmosphere grew increasingly tense as Atlas and Charity felt the military vehicles hot on their heels. Time tightened like a noose around their throats. Charity continued her panicked search for oxygen tanks, each movement an embodiment of the importance that came with the impending threat of suffocation. The repetitive beeping from the oxygen tanks served as a deadly countdown to their fate.

"Find oxygen, or we're going to suffocate to death!" Atlas's voice rang out. The father refused to succumb to the notion of giving up. Amid the seemingly endless road to nowhere, he found the desire to press on. He floored the Cybertruck, making the powerful vehicle surge forward as he pushed its limits. The constant beeping was a dire reminder of their mortality. Each electronic pulse echoed like Father Time, waiting to snatch his next victims, sending them into the abyss of the unknown.

The group of military vehicles closed in on the Cybertruck, their pursuit mirroring the poetic descent of vultures circling their prey. The barbaric nature of fear, deeply ingrained in humanity, was a trait that time had never been able to extinguish. The race against time unfolded, with the sands of life running out, each grain a maestro conducting the fatal orchestra.

Their predicament grew worse with each passing moment. No saviors lurked on the horizon. No miracle was going to emerge from the ailing world. The shrill beeping of their oxygen tanks became a drumbeat of oxygen deficiency, punctuated by a warning sound that echoed like a messenger of doomsday.

The daughter felt the mounting crisis take hold of her reality as anxiety tightened its grip on her mind. Her impending fate began to mount. The daughter gasped for air, her actions mirroring that of a diver trapped in the deep sea in desperate need of oxygen. She continued gasping for life, but the grasp of suffocation had already begun its embrace. Charity began to choke to death. Atlas glanced back and witnessed Charity's labored breaths turn into forceful gasps. Atlas slammed on the brakes, forcing the vehicle to an abrupt stop.

The Cybertruck screeched and skid to a stop. The pursuing military vehicles swiftly closed in and formed a tight circle around the immobilized vehicle. They created a perimeter that surrounded the vehicle from all possible angles. Inside, Atlas's frantic search for oxygen tanks became increasingly desperate, his hands rummaging through every corner as the time sensitive seconds ticked away. Charity's condition worsened. She clutched her throat, her eyes wide with panic as she silently pleaded with Atlas for help. The sound of her choking filled the space.

The soldiers unleashed a hail of gunfire from all angles, their shots reflected off the Cybertruck. The sturdy armor held strong against the metallic clings and clangs and provided a crucial shield against the crossfire. A soldier planted a *bomb* on the rooftop in the heart of the conflict.

Atlas's searching hands uncovered a concealed hatch on the floor. Without haste, he unlocked it, revealing a hidden compartment brimming with a stockpile of oxygen tanks. Atlas seized one of the tanks and rushed to Charity's side.

The father disconnected the depleted tank from her mask and swapped it for a fresh one. With nimble movements, Atlas secured a fresh oxygen tank to Charity, double-checking to ensure that the connections were airtight. As the tank activated with a subtle hiss, a stream of oxygen flowed into Charity's mask. Her labored breaths gradually stabilized, each inhale and exhale a mini victory. Atlas observed her safety and mentally took a deep breath of gratitude. A dash of hope rekindled within the shelter of their metal fortress for a moment. The gift of life in a world that offered none had been reestablished for the daughter.

Atlas hastily secured an oxygen tank to his back during their frantic escape. As the gunfire ceased, he heard the faint sound of the ticking timer mounted on the Cybertruck's roof. The ominous rhythm of the approaching threat propelled him into a wild search for a means of defense. By a stroke of luck, he stumbled upon a *machine gun*, clutching this fortunate discovery. "Get down!" His words, a final plea from the ticking bomb. Charity instinctively took cover as the world around them quaked in unease and anticipation of the forthcoming cataclysm. With a deafening *explosion*, the Cybertruck violently rocked and shook. The *detonation* tore through the roof. The force of the blast sent Atlas and Charity reeling, but they braced themselves tenaciously. A gaping gash on the roof exposed the intruding soldiers, who breached the vehicle. Thick plumes of smoke billowed, shrouding their vision in a blinding cloak of darkness.

Atlas took his position near the breach, prepared to face their assailants head-on. Charity seized a canteen and collected blood from a nearby barrel. Bullets tore through the vehicle as the father and daughter scrambled for cover, their sanctuary under attack. The father retaliated with rapid gunfire from the machine gun, eliminating a few soldiers with deadly accuracy like a guardian of life. He ducked back into the Cybertruck, protecting himself from retaliation. The soldiers scattered for cover; their instincts drove them to seek any advantages. One soldier clambered onto the roof, hoping to secure a calculated vantage point. The other soldiers moved away from the ruptured opening, regrouping for another assault from a different angle.

Atlas turned to his daughter, his voice tense. "Look for a way out," he commanded. Charity searched through the jumble of scattered supplies in the backseat, tossing items aside in her frenetic attempt to find an escape hatch.

The persistent soldier perched on the roof fired round after round, eventually penetrating the gap. Havoc engulfed inside as the bullets entered, the sound growing louder with each round. Death was closing in. Atlas crammed for cover. Charity found a hidden *escape hatch*. She gasped in relief then shouted, "Found something!" The enemy gunfire ceased. Atlas emerged through the hole in the roof, catching the soldiers off guard, and swiftly took down the one on the roof.

The remaining soldiers reacted quickly, their bullets finding the intended target. A bullet grazed Atlas's shoulder, causing him to wince in pain. He lowered himself back inside the Cybertruck. Although he was wounded, he was a warrior and could take the pain. Blood oozed down Atlas's arm like etched crimson. He remained focused on their escape. The father directed his attention towards the escape hatch.

Charity, with concern in her voice, spoke, "Dad, your arm!" Atlas ignored her reaction and reached for the latch that opened the escape hatch, revealing a *manhole cover* underneath the Cybertruck that led underground. The soldiers converged on the opening, their collective manpower fueling their pursuit.

Charity scurried down the ladder, entering the unknown. Atlas grabbed the shovel and followed closely behind his daughter. The sound of gunfire faded as he closed the manhole cover behind them. In the blinding darkness, Atlas and Charity ventured into an uncertain, underground future.

* * *

Beneath the fiery sky Atlas's breath labored as he took in air from his rusted tank. With his welder mask on, Atlas drifted into a haze of nothingness during the burial; he was forever a lost soul. During the silence, eight-year-old Charity observed with wordless contemplation, an oxygen mask securely covering her innocence. Every shovel's worth of dirt felt like an additional burden on Atlas's weary shoulders, and each scoop depleted his strength. The soil itself seemed to resist, as if to reflect his own mourning. His soulmate, Angelica, was gone, never to return. The man persevered, knowing there was no other path to take. He understood this was the end of a chapter in life. Like all souls who walk this Earth, no one is ever fully prepared to bid farewell to those they cherish at the end. Once the pit had reached its final depth, Atlas's breath came in—jagged and laborious. With admiration, he lowered the coffin into the earth; his gentle touch on the coffin revealed the weight of his memories. The coffin was not just a vessel for the departed but a sacred sanctuary. It held a love that could never be extinguished from his heart.

Exhausted and broken, Atlas crumbled to his knees, the unforgettable burden of loss presented him to the Earth. Tears emerged from his soul. Charity sensed her father's anguish. She approached cautiously, her small hand unshaken as it reached out to touch his shoulder. Her eyes, wide with concern, held a wisdom far beyond her years. In this moment, the child's guidance held the promise of peace.

Atlas, his spirit rekindled by the presence of his daughter, gathered her into his arms and held her close. Her small arms clung tightly to his neck as she sought comfort. Together, they departed the grave. Atlas carried his daughter away from his wife's tomb, their souls adrift in a sea of eternal darkness.

* * *

Earth, a forsaken orb, wobbled on its fragile axis, its celestial waltz with the sun nearing its mournful conclusion. Nightfall descended and immersed the world in shades of obscurity. From the quantum depths where particles whisper secrets known only to the cosmos, a subtle interplay unfolds. Solar winds engaged in their eternal waltz with the planet's atmosphere. The subatomic tango left traces of decay upon the world, a dance of disintegration.

Time witnessed the gradual erosion, both imperceptible and inevitable. Infinitesimal decay, where the particles of the world surrendered to entropy. The runaway greenhouse effect weakened Earth's atmosphere while the solar winds stripped the planet of its protective shield. Earth drifted into cosmic solitude, its story known only to the quantum secrets of space.

* * *

Deep within the Earth laid a labyrinthine cave system, its ancient passages a cryptic web of secrets waiting to be unraveled. The rock walls of this subterranean world echoed with tales of survival. In these underground catacombs, desperate souls took refuge during the apocalypse to escape the surface's deadly radiation from the sun after the atmosphere withered away. Ancient art etched upon the walls told stories of forgotten worlds. Vivid symbols spoke of lives lived from ancient days. Within the frigid depths of the underground labyrinth, Atlas and Charity navigated the chilling darkness. A distinctive bodysuit layer clung to their skin, a futuristic creation designed to shield them from solar radiation and regulate body temperatures as the shifting rhythms of the day played out on a radioactive planet. Atlas pushed forward, his footsteps an echo in the icy underworld. He handed Charity his trench coat, a helpful layer against the frozen tundra. "Put this on," he murmured. Atlas adjusted his oxygen tank, bit his teeth in the cold environment, and draped his jacket over Charity's small shoulders.

"What about you?" Charity asked with concern in her voice.

"I'll be fine," Atlas reassured her. He pulled his daughter closer, enfolding her in the warmth of his tattered jacket. The daughter embraced the added garment. "Better?" Atlas asked, a look of concern etched across his face. The father knew she was exhausted.

"A little bit," Charity replied.

They continued to wander through the extensive passageways of the cave for an escape route. A cruel amalgamation of exhaustion and dehydration took a heavy toll on Charity's frail body.

In the distance, a swooshing sound could be heard—a signal of flowing water concealed behind walls of impenetrable rock. The father and daughter pounded on the rocks to breach the ancient stone barriers. The unbeatable wall of nature mocked their efforts and denied them access to the water. Charity, bent over and gasped for air, her chest heaving. Atlas, spent, rested his head against the rock. Eventually, their struggles took their toll.

"Where's the water going?" Charity inquired, her curiosity piqued.

"It fluctuates underground, going deep into the core of Earth," Atlas replied. He knew of the persisting rumors that hidden beneath Earth's scorched surface, trapped in rocks and minerals, was an ocean larger than the one that once graced the planet's surface. Unfortunately, water underground had been imprisoned long before the inferno melted the water and remained an inaccessible treasure buried beneath the subterranean realm.

A faint pitter-patter sound resonated throughout the underground cave. Atlas remained stoic, his grip tightened around his pistol. He felt a presence close by. The torchlight continued to light their path as they rounded the corner. Awaiting them was a group of *dirty kids*, their faces concealed behind eerie *tribal Mayan masks*. The ancient masks had carvings and vibrant colors, their enigmatic expressions preserved the stories of forgotten generations. Eskimo-like garments hung from their skeletal frames, each wore an oxygen tank.

One kid, armed and masked, stepped forward, the barrel of his gun aimed directly at Atlas and Charity. Atlas slowly lowered his pistol. "We're just passing through." The kids, united, scrutinized the father and daughter with wary eyes, searching for any hint of deception. "Where's the way out?" Atlas commanded. The children's silence bred tension as the armed kid drew nearer.

He kept his gun aimed at the father and daughter, his masked face a chilling enigma. "We need your oxygen," the kid said with an intimidating tone.

"Not going to happen." The atmosphere grew denser and was charged with unspoken threats.

In a desperate act of goodwill, Charity produced a can of soup from her jacket pocket and extended it towards the armed kid. "Here. Eat something," she offered.

The armed kid seized the can and hurled it back to the ravenous group of starving children. Mayhem erupted as the kids fought over the can of soup. The armed kid cocked his gun with eyes focused on Atlas, his finger hovered over the trigger. "You have 10 seconds… 9… 8…" The kid raised his voice.

Charity wavered, losing her strength. Atlas watched his daughter collapse onto the ground, her body was suffering from exhaustion and dehydration. He rushed to her side and cradled her in his arms. Atlas removed a glove and placed his fingers against Charity's wrist. "Stay with me."

He detected a faint, steady pulse. A soft rhythm granted the father a moment of relief. "Strong girl." Atlas hoisted Charity onto his shoulder in a fireman's carry, her small form draped across his shoulders. His resolve was unbroken.

The kid spoke loudly, "We need your oxygen!"

Atlas was fearless in his response, "Shoot me." Atlas met the kid's hallow masked eyes, which reflected the spirit of a man who had traversed hell. Atlas walked away, carrying the responsibility of saving Charity.

The armed kid, torn between murder and humanity, hesitated—his finger trembled on the trigger. The other children goaded him on while the rest remain engrossed in their fight over the can of soup. Atlas faded into the shadows of the caves. A gunshot rattled off in the opposite direction of Atlas. In a last-minute act, the armed kid redirected his aim from Atlas to the children locked in their savage fight over the can of soup. The kid's gunshot rattled off the cave walls, shattering the tension.

Atlas strained himself as he pushed open the heavy manhole cover, emerging from the underground depths with Charity draped over his shoulder. The world above greeted them with an even colder climate, a frigid wind sliced through the air, leaving a shimmering frost upon the landscape. The arctic environment was so glacial that even Satan, frozen in the ancient epic poem of Dante's Inferno, would find it hard to endure. In Atlas's realm of purgatory, evil reigned supreme, but the man's spirit continued to drive him forward, defying the odds.

Atlas stumbled along the road. Each step remained a battle against the coldness of the environment. The freezing temperature sucked the energy from his body. The man pushed himself to the limits and refused to surrender to the forces that sought to break him.

Atlas took a few steps before his knees buckled and he collapsed onto the earth. He clutched his head to stop the pain. Blood seeped from his welder's mask, trickling from his ears. He had stumbled into the clutches of a divergent gravitational pressure field, a force that wreaked havoc on his body and left him at the mercy of its mysterious power. Variations in the pull of gravity remained hidden like whispered secrets of the Earth. Beneath the cracked crust of the planet, deep in its core, the sphere shifted and quivered, giving rise to subtle differences in the embrace of gravity. It was not a tale of fiction. These were the hushed murmurs of the Earth, where density and mass played their secret games. In the world's orchestration, the opera of rock and mineral, topography and time were the key players. From unseen magma chambers to the voices of buried rock, they held their secrets close, adding their weight to the tale of gravitation.

Atlas, fueled by an inner surge of energy, rose to his feet, a grueling effort against the force of gravity. Every step became an odyssey. Under the canopy of an inky-black sky, Atlas moved with persevering purpose. The stars, those ancient watchers of the cosmos, shimmered above, offering their light as his only guide. Atlas forged ahead with a challenge as though a boulder of the world were on his shoulders. His daughter held onto to him, her presence a constant reminder of the duty he carried upon his shoulders. The celestial constellations offered their ethereal diamond glow to lead him through the darkness.

It was their guidance that brought him to a *masonry structure*, a futuristic cave fortress that offered shelter. The structure's exterior, an assemblage of rugged rocks, allowed it to withstand the deadly environment. The man's desire to live burned fiercer and guided him forward. Even the hand of the devil, with all its malevolent might, could not stop him. The man would not falter. He would persist unless the fabric of an alternate universe was ripped apart by the hand of God to stop his journey. He pressed on, drawn toward the masonry structure like a moth to a flame. The front glass door entrance was propped open and welcomed the visitors in. Atlas entered the threshold into the unknown.

A disquieting silence gripped the man's soul as he stepped inside the fortress. The structure, far from inviting, seemed to await the arrival of the deceased. It was a relic from an era of primitive survival and wasn't designed for modern comfort. It was a barricade against the apocalypse. Soot smeared every surface. A trail of blood and footprints called Atlas deeper into the labyrinthine core of the stronghold.

Atlas advanced towards the kitchen; the stone walls showcased a brutal confrontation. The scattered bloodstains hinted at the ferocity of a struggle. On the frigid stone floor was a discarded bloodstained *ax*, a weapon of terror within the home.

On the kitchen counter, two wedding rings—drenched in blood—rested as gruesome mementos of a love forever torn apart. From the ceiling beams, a motionless skeleton swung with eerie grace. Nearby, a decaying skull, likely that of the wife, provided a chilling scene: An end of days Romeo and Juliet ritual. Suicide seemed to be the easier way for the departed husband and wife.

Embracing death as an old friend was a comfort most souls took advantage of during the apocalypse. The illusion of evading death, an artifact of ancient times when humanity still held aspirations, had withered into the dread of a world where mankind stood as captives on Earth. Fantasies of exoplanetary salvation remained trivial delusions. The Earth was only destined to be humanity's eternal home until they became extinct. Humanity's desire to abandon Earth in search of a new planet remained a dream unfulfilled. Interstellar travel posed an impossible obstacle. The riddles embedded within the fundamental forces of nature proved to be troublesome, ensuring that the obsession of escaping to another world would forever remain just a dream.

With impressive, reserved stamina, Atlas lowered Charity to the floor. The father scoured every nook and cranny, tearing through the hidden compartments and closets in his search for water. The fortress remained a barren well. Unzipping his survival bag, Atlas rushed back to his daughter's side. The father was determined to bring his daughter back to consciousness. He created a makeshift quarantine unit by positioning both of their heads inside the sack. Working quickly, he unhooked his oxygen apparatus and connected it to the sack, adjusting the settings to allow a steady flow of oxygen into their shared, enclosed space. With utmost care, he removed Charity's oxygen apparatus, allowing the pristine oxygen within their improvised shelter to nourish her weakened body. Their fates intertwined in this fragile bubble amidst the savage world outside. "Charity, wake up!" the father pleaded. The daughter remained in a deep state of unconsciousness. Atlas produced the canteen of blood, its crimson contents their current elixir of life, and he held it to Charity's lips. "Drink it!" he urged.

Charity moved ever so slightly as if her father's words resonated inside her psyche. Her subtle resistance was evident as she squinted in defiance. Atlas, driven by a primal instinct, forced her head towards the canteen, compelling her to drink the crimson elixir. Despite her faltering attempts to resist, she was no match for the strength of her father. "You have to drink the blood. We have no choice." The father felt immense guilt, his conscience hampered by the adversity his daughter had experienced. Survival had always been brutal throughout human history, from hunter gatherers to the Anthropocene epoch. Atlas understood he had to go to overwhelming lengths to rescue his precious daughter from the clutches of death in this land of evil. She drank as much blood as she could manage and slowly returned to the realm of the conscious. Atlas tenderly repositioned her oxygen apparatus and laid her on the ground. Traces of blood lingered on her parched lips.

"I'm sorry you have to live in this world," the father sheepishly said, his voice burdened with shame. Their journey toward the coast, an odyssey filled with uncertainty, had offered no promises or guarantees. The man grappled with his doubts, swallowing the emotions that threatened to submerge his soul.

Could this cave fortress become their final resting place, just as it had for ancient humans millions of years ago? He fought to suppress such treacherous thoughts, knowing they could lead him down the path of darkness.

Charity strained to hear her father's words. She lingered in the suffocating grasp of exhaustion, attempting to regain consciousness and claw her way back from her state of unconsciousness. Atlas put on his welder's mask, hooked up his oxygen apparatus, took a deep breath, and felt a sense of relief. He gently lifted Charity into his arms and carried her to the living room.

Atlas gently eased Charity onto a worn couch and carefully covered her with a threadbare blanket, adding another layer on top of his trench coat to shield her from the cold. She stirred slightly, a glimmer of improvement. It was evident that rest and time were her allies. The daughter's well-being was paramount no matter the cost. Blood continued dripping down Atlas's arm, his injury apparent.

Atlas took a moment to catch his breath and surveyed the black, dust-covered room. His body was bone-tired. He sat there for a moment. Rest remained a bona fide comfort that had long abandoned him during their quest. His weathered eyes fell on a globe of earth that rested on a nearby table. The globe's surface was obscured beneath a coat of ash, a reflection of the world's transformation. Atlas's fingers gingerly spun the globe, and he watched as it turned in slow, contemplative circles. The man became enchanted by the hypnotic rotation and sought a prophetic sign from the planet that had experienced humanity's rise and fall. In the quiet of the room, the world spun as Atlas's bloodshot eyes traced the earth. He wondered if salvation or damnation awaited them in this ever-turning sphere.

His voice, filled with a touching plea, broke the silence. He began to speak, not to the inanimate globe but to Earth itself. "You've witnessed it all, haven't you? The rise and fall of civilizations, the duality of humanity's nature. And now, here we are, on the brink of extinction. We should have protected you." His voice quivers with the remorse of unspoken regrets. The man stared deep into the globe, a God of nature. "Can you help us? I'll never doubt you again. Don't let our species die like this. We deserve better. Not all of us are monsters. Show me a miracle." The quiet Earth, a humble witness to the helplessness of its own creation. "You never answer…" he said as his shoulders slumped. The man pondered that miracles were nothing more than constructs of human imagination, ephemeral illusions.

Without warning, the basement door creaked open, a sudden intrusion into Atlas's moment of serenity. His instincts snapped him out of his trance. He abandoned the globe and left it behind as he retreated, swift and cautious, back towards the kitchen.

Atlas's fingers tightened around the pistol; his every muscle coiled in anticipation as he aimed it at the ominous figure that emerged from the depths of the basement. His heart pounded in his chest and his breaths were slow and measured. As the figure came into view, Atlas's eyes narrowed; he recognized the familiarity of a *rover*. Its design was reminiscent of the early exploratory machines that roamed the surface of Mars. Those robots were introduced as in-home security systems during the environmental collapse, specifically guarding the homes of owners. These machines, symbols of curiosity for the discovery of the universe, had transformed into instruments of surveillance and was a regretful memento of how the world had changed. *Bing!* A deafening ring shattered the silence as the rover's metallic voice punctuated the air with an intrusive sound. "Intruder alert!" the rover's artificial intelligence system shrieked.

In an instant, the tranquility was shattered. *Bang!* A gunshot was fired from the rover as the bullet tore through the air, narrowly missing Atlas as he ducked for cover behind the countertop. What followed was a deadly dance, a perpetual cat-and-mouse game played out in the kitchen. A game of survival between man and machine. Atlas swiftly concealed the pistol, his mind a battleground of strategy as he assessed the layout of the room.

Atlas climbed onto the kitchen counter and seized the ax. Positioned strategically, he readied himself to spring over the rover and into the fray. In a daring leap, Atlas jumped off the counter, his body a blur as the ax descended with a resounding chop onto the rover's robotic weapon system components. The clash of metal against metal filled the room, each swing of the ax a thunderous declaration of defiance. *Cling! Clang!* Echoes resounded as metal fragments broke away. The rover's invincible frame began to crumble beneath the intense assault. With a final, cataclysmic strike, the rover exploded into a chaotic burst of shattered pieces.

Atlas stood over the debris, his chest heaving and sweat-soaked as he trembled from the adrenaline surge. The battle was won, but the cost became apparent as the punishing events of the day piled on him. Atlas was only a man. Overwhelmed by exhaustion, he collapsed to his knees. His body was battered but victorious. Triumphant, yet he knew that the battle remained infinite. The man wondered how much longer he could endure before being consumed by Father Time. Atlas caught sight of a neglected *piano* nestled in the corner of the room and walked towards it. He swept away the layers of dust that gathered on the forgotten instrument.

Atlas sat on the dusty bench and placed his fingers on the keys. He started to play, his touch gentle and commanding. The music weaved an abundance of emotions, binding together moments of triumph, sadness, and the distant echo of hope. While the notes danced upon the air, Atlas found comfort in the familiar embrace of the piano, an oasis of peace. The haunting beauty of the music transcended and reached into the deepest parts of his fractured soul.

Charity stirred slightly and subtly fluttered her eyelids. The soft melody, like a lullaby from another life, gently guided her back into an awake state. A smile crossed her lips. In the daughter's dream, she ventured into a past life, where the soothing strains of a piano whispered forgotten memories.

* * *

In a different time, illuminated in the soft, warm glow of candlelight, a harmonious trio gathered around the piano. Atlas, Angelica, and a young Charity were together as their fingers danced across the keys in perfect synchrony. A graceful utopia before their world unraveled.

* * *

Atlas's hands moved with fierce passion across the piano, his bloodied gloves smeared the ivory keys as he played with an intensity born of turmoil. He was lost in the moment, a man possessed by the beauty of the music.

The notes poured forth from the piano, a vortex of raw emotions channeled through his skillful fingers. Music, a manifestation of creation, paved the way for the birth of life since the dawn of time. Atlas began his finale, accelerating the tempo… picking up the pace… pushing it even faster… until he concluded his performance. The man lowered his head in a deep meditation. In the late hours of the night, danger finally seemed to rest. But the man understood all too well that these illusions were nothing more than a temporary moment from the inevitable tempest of chaos that lurked and waited for its opportunity to strike.

When it is obvious that the goals cannot be reached, don't adjust the goals, adjust the action steps.
Confucius

Please guide all beings from this swamp of cyclic existence!
Tibetan Book of the Dead

HOPE

*You cannot get through a single day without having an
impact on the world around you. What you do makes a
difference, and you have to decide what kind of a difference
you want to make.*
Jane Goodall

* * *

Earth persisted in its lonesome voyage throughout the cosmos, a little brown dot adrift in the unending void. Its orbit around the sun was a universal act of proficiency. The sun continued in its assault upon the atmosphere. Solar winds breached the dying atmosphere, an invasion of entropy. Reality reclaimed what was rightfully theirs and knew no obstacle could delay its uncompromising advance.

* * *

Icicles stood frozen against the glass, creating a spiderweb of patterns. Symmetric and antisymmetric designs pervaded the windows. Atlas sat on the edge of the couch and stared at the window's icy designs.

Metaphorical implications ran through the man's thoughts. Atlas navigated a network of uncertainties. He was never quite certain of what lay beyond each twist and turn. The only hope he had was a promise of a new beginning. His eyes, filled with exhaustion, settled upon his daughter who slept peacefully.

The distant howling of the wind, a mournful ghost, served as an echo of the departed souls. Its howling carried the voices of countless lives lost, a requiem of death. "Earth's orbit remains constant around our sun," Atlas remarked with a tinge of philosophical thought. The wind's wrath intensified; its magnitude shook the foundations of the masonry structure.

Tremors created a meteorological occurrence far beyond what could have been considered ordinary in this surreal landscape. "Sometimes," Atlas began, "I wish the sun would die, bringing an end to our suffering… but nature endures on this forsaken world."

The horizon vanished beneath an approaching wall of swirling dust, a monstrous *dust storm*. Earth's dust storms had morphed into Mars-like superstorms, drawing comparisons to their planetary counterpart. Both worlds were united in their shared turmoil. A phenomenon began to unfurl, reminiscent of the tornado that whisked Dorothy away to the Land of Oz.

Quickly, Atlas woke up Charity from her sleep. "We have to leave!" Charity watched in awe at the approaching storm, an elemental force that threatened to engulf everything in its path. The father and daughter hastily gathered their belongings and made a swift exit from the rock fortress.

Atlas and Charity scrambled into the cab of a *semi-truck,* its back end cargo container was missing. With a determined twist of the key, the engine awakened, its roar filled the air as it came to life. Atlas shifted gears and accelerated as the tires gripped the road in their mad rush to escape. The vortex's rage reached its crescendo, a juggernaut of annihilation. It hurled debris with cruel intent, each projectile a dangerous product from Mother Nature. The storm picked up in intensity and momentum, closing its distance with the truck. The dust storm grew larger until it loomed over the semi-truck.

A rush of wind surged into the semi-truck. Atlas clutched the wheel as the vehicle shuddered under the assault. The storm's temper threatened to tear it apart. Atlas remained vigilant, steering away from the crucible of the storm. A powerful gust tore apart the ancient stone masonry structure, reducing it to a vestige of its former self. Charity looked out the rear window, her eyes focused on the devastation.

The truck rumbled along the road. The blizzard of gray ash swirled and twirled. In the sky, a whirlwind of

Halloween-esque colors—fiery hues that seemed to devour the horizon—painted a surreal portrait.

Atlas noticed Charity was lost in her thoughts as she looked at the inferno sky and said, "Any dreams." Recalling dreams became the daughter's only escapism. In the depths of the night, when the world was asleep, she would return to the safety of her dreams where possible impossibilities were amplified, and their challenging existence momentarily lifted. In those moments, the daughter could escape the brutality of their journey and find peace in the realm of imagination, if only for a moment.

Charity's mind drifted back into the depths of recollection, "I was standing at the edge of a beach; waves were crashing against the shore. Then I went swimming in the ocean. The strangest part was, I could breathe underwater. The water felt like oxygen... And I saw people, swimming together, smiling and laughing. It was a perfect day."

The father had devoured countless books about water throughout his lifetime. To him, it had been a God, a fantastical narrative of a time when civilizations flourished. The man couldn't help but find his thoughts drifting to what might have been in a past that now seemed like a distant, unreachable dream. He'd often pondered the sensation of swimming in the ocean, a concept close to a miracle in his eyes.

"They say humans have always had a deep connection with the ocean. It's supposed to be calming," he mused. For a moment, the father and daughter were connected through this speculation. A twinkle of possibilities in a world where such moments were gone. The hypnotic dance of the surreal ash held them in its melancholic spell. They were entranced by the allure of the past. The thought of an enchanting ocean was nothing more than a rich gift for their minds. Their enchantment ended by an ear-splitting sound that pulsated through the dystopian wasteland. Their dream was fractured, a deception of normalcy gone.

Two *sand buggies* tore through the road, the drivers wearing futuristic spacesuits. An *individual* in a *gravity jet suit* soared through the air, their gun unleashing an excess of bullets. The sand buggies moved with calculated precision, attempting to corner the truck from divergent angles. The pursuit was tenacious. In these times, a functioning vehicle with working mechanical parts was as coveted as gold had been during the pioneering days. This tribe embarked on a hunt to secure one.

The truck careened through the road, a race for survival against pursuers who closed in with dangerous intent. Fueled by their desire to outrun their assailants, the truck hurtled toward the wide opening of an *underground tunnel.* The truck began its descent into the depths of Earth.

These tunnels—initially conceived as an innovative solution to the automobile-induced overpopulation and a gateway for underground CO2 capture. Now nothing more than an artifact of humanity's inability to curb its voracious appetite for the overconsumption of fossil fuels. The tunnel's darkness beckoned. The pursuers, undeterred by the daunting tunnel, followed. Their pursuit knew no bounds. They plunged into the subterranean depths, their presence echoing through the maze of underground passages.

The earth's dark blood seeped underground, a trickle of its abundant fossil wealth. Its glory, a distant memory, that had held society in its grip. Those days were but a vanished dream in a world changed. Amidst the echoing gunfire, the air grew heavy with the acrid stench of burning oil, explosive dangers that encircled them. The ground was a treacherous sea of oil surrounded by the pursuers who fired rounds from every direction. Atlas and Charity ducked inside the truck, narrowly evading the bullets that whizzed over their heads. The shots cracked the windshield.

Atlas unlocked the driver's side door as the pursuit closed in behind them. "Take the wheel!" he commanded. Charity seized control, her hands gripped the wheel as she focused. Atlas swung the driver's side door wide open and used it as a shield as he reached for an overhead handle inside the truck. He hung his body outside the cab and positioned himself into a firing position. Bullets ripped through the air around him. Glass shattered and oil splashed. Charity kept the truck on course. She floored the gas pedal and picked up more speed by the second. Black smoke billowed from the truck's engine. The exchange of gunfire escalated, forcing Atlas to abandon his post and heroically jump into the truck's rear compartment to obtain a better vantage point in a face off against the gravity jet suit individual.

Smash! The truck collided with brutal force into the leading sand buggy, sending it hurtling into the tunnel wall. Amid the thick smoke, the gravity jet suit individual maneuvered with astonishing agility. Atlas lined up his focus with the pistol and pulled the trigger. His well-aimed shot found its mark, sending the gravity jet suit individual hurtling earthward. With a resounding *crash*, they collided with the ground, no longer a formidable presence in the pursuit. The second sand buggy faced a similar fate as Atlas took aim with skilled precision at their tires. Bullets ripped through the rubber, causing the sand buggy to convulse and somersault through the air before merging with the rocky ground. All pursuers were eliminated.

The truck surged out of the underground tunnel. Ahead, the road stretched into an uncertain horizon. Atlas reentered the passenger's side of the truck's cab.

"Nice driving."

"I learned from the best."

Atlas spotted something in the distance, an abandoned desert road. "Take this road, shortcut to the coast," he instructed, his words measured with strategic intent. Charity turned the wheel and guided the truck down the rugged path, sending dust swirling into the barren air. Atlas took a sip from the canteen of blood, its iron flavor a last resort for hydration. He offered it to Charity.

"You have to stay hydrated."

"I don't want to."

"You're going to die if you don't."

Charity eased up, removed her oxygen mask, and took a sip from the canteen. The taste of life. The blood's metallic tang lingered in Charity's mouth. She glanced ahead and noticed a sparkle on the horizon of the sun's fading rays.

The truck continued forward, revealing a surreal avant-garde metropolis known as *Epoch City*, an anomaly in the middle of nowhere. Epoch City authentically intended to be the hope of salvation for cities across the globe, a vision of a metropolitan city that could sustain itself entirely through green energy. The city's architecture defied convention, with buildings stacked haphazardly, some seemingly suspended upside down. The cityscape resembled a bewildered Rubik's Cube of solar panels, a cryptic jigsaw puzzle waiting to be solved by those who dared to enter its domain.

The man's eyes drifted across the unusual cityscape, an intricate mesh of clean energy innovation. Atlas read intensely about the subject over the years. In his eyes, he saw the limitations. He understood that while Epoch City was a step towards sustainability, it's only a fraction of the greater puzzle. The real challenge was in finding a way to exist with fossil fuels, perhaps in the elusive realm of carbon capture, or in other uncharted territories that held the promise of a true solution.

In the end, Atlas understood the paradoxical riddle that living without fossil fuels was impossible. Every whimsical aspect of reality, including the foundations of propulsion and engineering, were intricately entwined with the realm of fossil fuels. Over the years, he had pondered the eternal limitations inherent in the laws of nature, and it became evident that the main roadblock was clearly the absence of innovation. The secret key was discovering a way for humanity to coexist with fossil fuels. In the shadow of Epoch City, fields of *nuclear fusion* and *fission reactors*, their eerie architecture was a reminder of humanity's desperate struggle to harness the elemental forces of creation and destruction. Despite humankind's aspirations, promises of nuclear fusion and fission remained unfulfilled worldwide, prevented by the insurmountable constraints of scientific ambition.

"Why is it built that way?"

"This city believed clean energy was the answer."

"Where is everybody?"

"Dead… Drive faster."

Epoch City, a modern-day Atlantis, remained a ghostly vestige of a civilization consumed by the apocalypse. This former empire, like the rest of the world, met its fate and succumbed to the runaway greenhouse effect. The truck hurtled onward, leaving behind the enigmatic city, its skyline vanishing on the horizon. The sky stretched boundlessly overhead, a mammoth skyline of raging red and orange. Beneath the truck's tires, the desert terrain rolled away in a monotonous rhythm.

Until a phantasmagorical anomaly became emergent. Gravity, the force that binds all to the planet, the universe's glue, had diverged. The truck was yanked off the ground. It hovered in the air, suspended in defiance of nature's rules, and dangled in a realm of weightlessness. A picturesque image presented itself, depicting a future where flying automobiles were foreseen. Rather than technology blazing the trail, it was the enigmatic gravitational phenomenon that paved the way to this unearthly reality.

Atlas and Charity exchanged bewildered glances as they grasped the bizarre event that seized their world. Inside the truck's cabin, the silence was deafening. The engine's growl had vanished, leaving only the soft hum of electronics. The objects within the cab float defined gravity's shackles.

"Dad, what's happening!?"

"Gravity!"

Perpetually, the truck glided effortlessly through the sky, carried by the invisible hand of destiny. It moved with a newfound freedom, unchained from the earthly constraints of physics. The truck levitated like a ghost against the backdrop of the endless desert, a surreal suspension. It contorted with unnatural grace, while rocks and sand remained trapped in mid-air, frozen in an otherworldly moment.

Atlas grappled with the unfathomable experience. They were thrust into a realm where the laws of existence had morphed into an unstable paradox. Their survival depended on swift adaptation to the mysteries of their planet's transformation. Charity's grip tightened on the steering wheel, her eyes focused on the unending road leading toward the edge of a mountain. Atlas peered out the window and spotted a *cliff* extending into the distance. The pull of gravity grew stronger, accelerating the truck's forward motion with each passing moment. Atlas reached across his daughter and grasped the driver-side door handle, pulling it open. Rushing wind whipped through the cabin of the truck as everything moved in a helter-skelter, reckless motion.

"We have to jump!"

"I can't do this!"

"Yes, you can! Go!"

Charity looked out the open door, the ground below blurring into a dizzying frenzy of motion.

"Now!" Atlas commanded.

Charity thrust herself into the void, her figure suspended in mid-air. She hovered, a breath away from the ground. Her limbs flailed to regain mastery over her body. Dread consumed her as the realization took hold: Gravity had abandoned its loyal duty. Her weak efforts to regain control resulted in chaotic somersaults. Her body was devoid of stability as the force of gravity exerted its influence, gradually pulling and tugging her backward, edging her closer to the cliff's edge. The entire sequence drew a comparable resemblance to the expansion rate of the universe. An odyssey where the edges of the cosmos could never truly be reached, an eternal horizon forever eluding the dynamic boundary conditions.

Atlas observed the harrowing battle his daughter waged against gravity. Without hesitation, he propelled himself from the truck, the rope-tethered shovel slung over his shoulder. In an instant, he was caught by the same weightlessness environment, his body spiraling in disorienting turmoil. Atlas stretched his arms toward his daughter, a frantic effort to bridge the expanding gap as she continued tumbling head over heels. The father's muscles strained until he transitioned into a freestyle swim, moving him closer through the air. It was difficult for Atlas to gain traction or control his movements, but the father refused to give up. He twisted and turned his body and used his arms and legs to fight against the opposing force, striving to align himself with Charity's trajectory. He managed to synchronize his movements with hers, inching closer with each passing second.

The truck bolted towards the edge of the cliff, plunging into the abyss below in a vigorous *nosedive*. Atlas stretched out his hand. He finally managed to grab Charity's hand. With his hand firmly clasped around hers, Atlas exerted his strength and attempted to pull her towards him in the face of the unpredictable forces at play. Gravity overtook Atlas and Charity, sending them into a *free fall* over the edge, their bodies tumbling in a wild descent. They held onto each other's hands with a vice-like grip in the midst of the terrifying plunge. Ensnared by an overwhelming force, their bodies were subjected to an irresistible tug. The ground surged upward with alarming velocity, expanding in size, while the world around them contorted into a display of distorted colors and shapes. They descended toward the ground, steadily nearing their destination.

Splash! They found themselves dropping into a river of viscous, black *oil*. The impact of their descent sent shockwaves through the inky liquid, causing it to roil and coil around their bodies. They struggled to orient themselves. Oil stuck to every movement, making it impossible to move fluidly. They battled this monstrous antagonist that wanted to drown them into the depths of oblivion.

Atlas swam his way through the dense oil. His limbs worked in perfect unison to navigate the fossil fuel currents. Here, hesitation and error were not a luxury afforded. The father treaded oil, slowly making his way toward his daughter. It felt as though he swam through the Higgs field of reality itself. A realm that granted mass upon particles, comparable to the viscosity of molasses. Amidst the encompassing darkness, he reached out to Charity, her existence submerged in purgatory. His arm encircled her, offering a rescue attempt that would never waver. The father wrapped his arms around his daughter, their bond reminiscent of a lifeguard's desperate rescue in turbulent waters. Only this was no ocean, but a sea of oil. In this surreal environment, their connection remained unbroken in the heart of the fossil fuel river.

The father swam harder with superhuman-like powers as his daughter held tightly onto him as they pressed on through the macabre current. Their journey seemed without end; the suffocating liquid tenacious in its quest to drag them under.

After what felt like an eternity of struggle, they arrived at the border of the oil river. With downright determination, they clawed their way onto the solid ground, escaping the wrath of the oil.

Atlas and Charity laid side by side, slowly rolling onto their backs, taking a rare pause to gather themselves. Their bodies were drenched and encrusted with the thick, black substance. Two weary wanderers in a world that wanted to kill them. The father shifted his focus back to Charity. Her breathing was rapid, devouring her oxygen reserves with a reckless urgency. Atlas reached for her hand. "Control your breathing," he whispered, the words hanging in the air.

Charity nodded in acknowledgment. Her exhausted breaths gradually subsided, the tempo a more measured, calculated rhythm. The father had always grappled with the paradox of oil and innovation. He knew for a technological civilization to progress, oil was essential. The father recognized that oil, for all its complexities and drawbacks, remained a necessary component. In a world evolving at an exponential pace, this resource was equally important.

Humanity failed in its attempt to find unorthodox ways to coexist with this black, ambivalent substance that powered technological advancements while acknowledging its profound impact on the planet. "We should have done better and found a way to live with oil. To respect it," Atlas spoke, his voice resonating with a sense of remorse for the failure of humanity.

Atlas ascended from the rugged terrain, rising with the determination of a heavyweight boxer who had stepped into the ring for the championship bout. His gestures were slow and measured as he reclaimed the shovel. The weight of the tool felt heavier and carried the importance of its destined purpose, resting upon his shoulder like a silent emblem of hope. The rope bound the shovel to him. His pistol glistened with the gloss of oil, its previous function rendered obsolete. Atlas tucked it into his waistband anyways. "We have to start walking."

"Where?"

Atlas, his gloved hand smeared with the stain of oil, gestured downstream, indicating the seemingly never-ending river of crude that stretched into the distance. His eyes fixed on the distant, uncertain horizon, where the river vanished into a hazy horizon. His voice was weathered and gruff. "The coast," he declared, his words resonating with confidence. But the daughter knew the formidable challenges ahead.

"We're never going to make it," she whispered, her voice trembling with the daunting truth that was before them. Their pursuit toward the elusive coast seemed an insurmountable odyssey.

Charity's pupils drifted downward, her eyes veiled by an unmistakable weariness. Seated at the edge of the oil river, her form anchored in the oil, she appeared as a lone figure beneath the oppressive weight of their challenge. The unforgiving world had etched its toll deeply into her. Her shoulders slumped with physical and emotional exhaustion. Words remained unspoken; there was no language left to articulate the depths of her mind.

Atlas extended his hand towards Charity. Her spirits were dampened. Doubts circled her mind amidst a flicker of fight still burning. She grasped her father's hand, their hands intertwined. The daughter stood up from the oily ground.

"We're close."

"Close to what?"

"A new life."

"There's nothing left! Look around! Does it look like life wants to keep existing?"

"You're not finished…"

Atlas pressed onward, his thoughts clouded in the secrets of their future. He was keenly aware that more danger awaited them. The man also knew he had a promise to uphold. A commitment that he would never surrender. He would never sit around and wait to die, no matter the circumstances. He squinted at the endless desert, a horizon where the sun's harsh rays met the earth's parched surface.

In the depths of his contemplation, he mused that in life, sometimes, all one could do was move forward. In the end, it was movement that created existence. With each heavy step, Atlas—the prophet of hope—advanced into the unknown. All that broke the silence was the haunting sound of the oil river slushing downstream, an ebony serpent weaving its way through the Earth.

Charity's aqua eyes, a rare glimmer of color amidst the monochrome desolation, were drawn into a hypnotic trance by her father's determination. A surge of willpower coursed through Charity's being, igniting a fire in her soul. The daughter had suddenly sparked a roaring blaze within her heart. She picked herself up from the oily ground and ran, her feet pounding. Her sprint towards her father a declaration to her unbroken spirit. Charity had an unquenchable desire to conquer the world they traversed.

Atlas, relieved by Charity's sudden surge of energy, turned his head to find her sprinting towards him. Her breathless words, sincere and heartfelt, cut through the silence. "You looked lonely," she panted. A faint, weary smile slowly creased the corners of Atlas's lips. He wrapped his arm around Charity's shoulders, drawing her close. Wrapped in each other's embrace, they pressed on. No more words passed between them, for none were necessary. They found peace in each other's presence, trekking forward in their epic search for another home.

* * *

The ocean, prodigious and untamed, stretched out to infinity. The sun hung low on the vista, casting a molten path across the water's surface. Waves, like the breath of some ancient Leviathan, surged and fell. Their white-capped peaks reflected the golden light of day. The salt-laden breeze, heavy with the secrets of the deep, swept over the shore, rustled the dunes, and carried the distant call of seagulls.

Beneath the surface, a vibrant reality teemed with life and color. Schools of fish moved in shimmering unison, their scales catching the light and refracting it into a dazzling array of hues. Coral reefs, delicate as lace, unfurled in unique patterns, sheltering a multitude of creatures, a diversity of life in this aqueous realm.

Farther out, the ocean extended into a mesmerizing spectacle, its depths an intoxicating blue that signaled the promise of unknown possibilities. The rhythm of the waves was a heartbeat of the unending cycle of life. A world of wonder.

* * *

Atlas and Charity pushed forward as the searing desert sun grew more intense. The inferno in the sky created a glow across the badlands. Before them a field of decrepit *solar panels* and *windmills* stretched for one hundred miles. These antiques were ancient artifacts, their solar surfaces covered in layers of sand. Once symbols of a valiant attempt at a cleaner energy future, they now represented the limitations of innovation. Sand veiled the innovations, the ancient desert covered the solar panels and windmills, creating fairy tales of a better future etched in grains of time. Unfortunately, these pioneering solutions fell short in matching the immense energy output of fossil fuels and were burdened by a multitude of quantitative challenges that dimmed the prospects of clean energy.

Atlas held knowledge of this technology, and with that knowledge came an acute awareness of the web of issues it presented. From Charity's perspective, she pondered humanity's past endeavors to harness solar energy in a bid to combat the runaway greenhouse effect. The daughter reflected on the inherent task that had plagued this technological pursuit. Her readings had unveiled a logical truth: While this innovative approach aimed to address environmental concerns, it had fallen short in providing a truly equitable and viable alternative to fossil fuels. It left many regions without equal access to the energy they so desperately needed.

"Why didn't people believe Earth would be unlivable in the future?" Charity mused.

"A few did," Atlas replied, his voice carrying the impact of understanding. "They were outnumbered. Humanity believed it would take thousands of years for the consequences to catch up."

"Wouldn't they want to stop the drought when they knew it would happen eventually?" Charity questioned.

"Some humans tried, but our innovation failed. Most leaders who ruled the world didn't feel the impact of their actions during their lifetime. There wasn't enough urgency, before it was too late," Atlas explained, revealing the reality of the apocalypse.

"That simple?" Charity's astonishment was evident.

"Unfortunately…"

"That sucks."

The heat waves continued to rise and fall from the seared earth, conjuring mirages of wavering peaks and valleys in the everlasting distance. The inferno desert displayed no compassion, its ferocity escalating. Atlas and Charity pressed onward, similar to Moses who guided the enslaved Jewish population out of the oppressive rule of Egypt. The world surrounding them appeared to shrivel and fade beneath the tenacious attack from our planet's star. Under this boiling assault, they trudged forward through the sweltering desert.

From over the blazing horizon, sand twirled in the air, and a *planetary rover* emerged over a field of jagged boulders. Its monstrous, sleek form navigated the desert, a bizarre traveler in this scorched realm. During the apocalypse, planetary rovers became the last resort, following the catastrophic runaway greenhouse effect. In certain regions, where traditional means of transportation had become impossible, these robust vehicles were the only means of travel. They provided humanity with means of mobility.

Atlas's fingers clenched around the oil-soaked pistol, lifting it in a defensive stance as the planetary rover approached. The rover's design contributed to the dreamlike unreality of the moment, a collision of worlds that seemed impossible. It halted just a stone's throw from Atlas and Charity, its engine humming with a serene softness. The vehicle's otherworldly aesthetics deepened the surreal nature of their encounter.

As the rover's door creaked open, a mystifying *driver*, obscured behind an *alien gas mask*, motioned for Atlas and Charity to step inside. Atlas maintained the pistol aimed squarely at the enigmatic driver, a gesture of caution in this unpredictable confrontation. "How you folks doing?" the driver asked.

"Why did you stop?" Atlas questioned.

"I wanted to offer some assistance," the driver gently offered. The driver let out a muffled chuckle. His emotions remained hidden beneath the supernatural mask. The laugh lingered, a pleasant reminder of humanity's capacity for humor.

"Nobody offers assistance anymore," Atlas responded, his uncertainty noticeable.

"That might be true, but I'm not like the others," the driver replied, their voice carrying an air of trustworthiness that was hard to ignore.

"Prove it."

"I'm not armed."

The driver stepped out from the planetary rover, his every movement unhurried, a clear signal of his understanding of the need for caution. He executed a slow, deliberate pivot, showing he had no weapons. Atlas exchanged a brief, unspoken connection with Charity. Their eyes conveyed the tension of trust. "Stay alert," Atlas cautioned. He never wavered, keeping his pistol trained on the driver as they approached the rover. The father's eyes locked onto something within and caught the glint of a water bottle. "Where's the water from?" he inquired, his voice tinged with wariness.

"Our well."

"Don't lie to us."

The driver continued his explanation. "My family has been fortunate during the apocalypse. You two are more than welcome in our village."

Atlas regarded the driver with skepticism. "Village? Everything is dead."

The driver, undeterred, offered reassurance. "Not with our fingerprints." The man contemplated whether humanity could endure as a united force. It was a question that had occupied his mind for countless years, even while he himself had managed to persist throughout.

Atlas shifted his eyes to Charity, their eyes locking in a connection of shared pessimism and cautious optimism. The driver's assertion of a surviving civilization was compelling. "How's that possible?" Atlas questioned, his uncertainty lingering.

"Lower that gun and let me show you," the driver urged, his words carrying a persuasive tone. Atlas was at the crossroads of a life-altering decision, his thoughts a tumultuous sea of uncertainty. He faced a perilous choice: To take a leap of faith and trust the driver, or face the relentless desert, their fate sealed by the merciless grip of dehydration. With reluctance gnawing at his being, Atlas lowered the pistol, his fingers unclenching from their tense grip on the weapon. He stared at the driver who extended an open hand, a symbol of trust.

171

The father pondered the risks and rewards. Cautiously, he accepted the driver's hand, a wordless pact to embark on this uncertain pursuit of possible salvation. "I'm a friend... Let's get out of this heat," the driver spoke, his words carrying a dignified reassurance that resonated in the scorching vastness of their surroundings.

The driver's steps carried him back to the rover. Atlas and Charity watched, their bodies drenched in oil, as the sun pounded on them. The ultimate decision loomed, leaving them no alternative but to seize this slender opportunity. The inferno desert would claim them, sooner rather than later. Recognizing this reality, both Atlas and Charity followed the driver's lead and boarded the rover, leaving behind the blazing sand dunes to embrace the questionable rescue.

The rover hummed along, its wheels traversing the drylands of earth. Inside, the air carried an intense but potentially hopeful camaraderie. Inside the insulated rover, the atmosphere became breathable, relieving Atlas, Charity, and the driver from the need to wear their oxygen apparatus. The sudden rush of fresh, unfiltered air was welcomed with relief. The driver's eyes, aged and brimming with empathy, shifted between Atlas and Charity, two weary wanderers he had welcomed into his secretive realm. The older Indian man's serene demeanor was akin to that of a monk deep in meditation. His face was concealed beneath a bandana mask as he extended the water bottle.

"Please, drink," he offered, a gesture of compassion. Charity's fingers closed around the water bottle, her throat parched and yearning for the miracle it held. She eagerly took a long drink, the cool liquid soothed her dehydrated body. It was a lifeline among the arid wilderness.

Atlas, pressing for answers, inquired, "How are humans surviving in your village?"

The driver, countering with a sense of wisdom forged by experience, responded, "We've discovered unity in these dire times, much like the tales of old. You've read about those days, haven't you?"

Atlas nodded, a sparkle of recognition in his eyes. The stories of a world where people lived in harmony with nature were almost mythical in the desolation they now wandered. Atlas remembered reading about tales of the past when humans reveled in the simple joys of nature, finding peace in the rustling leaves and the sweet chirping of birds. Those stories seemed as relevant as religious mythological tales in his eyes. Those stories were distant echoes of a world that had slipped away from the grasp of humanity. Atlas put his undivided interrogation skills on the driver. "What do you eat?" Atlas asked.

The man confidently responded, "We grow vegetable and raise livestock." The driver, his eyes ancient pools of knowledge, redirected his attention to Charity, who sat with fatigue etched into every line of her young face. His gaze was gentle, understanding the difficulties she carried on her battle-tested shoulders. "You've seen things, haven't you?"

"I've had better days."

The driver nodded, acknowledging the pain that hid beneath her words. There was no need for further explanation. They shared a mutual understanding, connected by the obstacles of what it meant to survive in these times. "Understandable. We've all had our share of dark moments."

The rover forged ahead into the unknown as the sun descended, entering night. Darkness settled around them, the world transformed, and the stars above twinkled like unremembered dreams. The father, the daughter, and their unconventional guide occupied the vehicle in contemplative silence, their thoughts meandering through the diversity of their individual experiences. The driver's gaze remained steady on the road, a road promising a new beginning. They all shared a glance, telling tales of the hardships they had weathered, pondering uncharted possibilities.

Simultaneously as the miles stretched on, Atlas contemplated the notion of fate. To him, it was an intriguing concept, a belief in something that surpassed the mechanics of logic. Fate, an invisible hand guiding the course of our lives, wove together complicated events, forever obscured in mystery.

The rover ventured deeper into the valley, cloaked beneath the ominous clouds of ash. Towering mountains flanked their path and created an imposing corridor, like the valley of the shadow of death. They neared the village nestled within the valley and an unfolding scene came into view. Small shacks, crafted from scavenged materials, were shoulder to shoulder, forming a close-knit community. The enduring spirit of humanity in the face of overwhelming devastation was portrayed. Above this resilient settlement, the massive *quarantine dome* resembled an arena. Its monumental presence stood in contrast to the ancient magnificence of the Roman Colosseum. Its translucent surface held an otherworldly glamour, enveloping the village. The sight before them resembled a vision of a futuristic Martian settlement, but it was firmly rooted on Earth. This engineering marvel, the dome, survived the environmental collapse. It shielded the village and provided a sanctuary of a purified civilization, allowing order and control for humanity. A vision obsessively desired on Mars, the dream of a flourishing and sustainable environment, ended up becoming a reality on Earth.

Under the dome, inhabitants went about their daily routines, every face remained concealed behind bandit masks. The masks had an air of mystique, satisfying a sort of weird cult attire. An occult *forest* had been nurtured and grown. Gargantuan trees with their colossal trunks reached towards the promised land, their canopy of leaves created a reservation of serenity. Beneath the cathedral of ancient evergreens, where moss-draped limbs embraced the whispers of eternity, the vibrant pulse of the magical forest unfolded. In the dappled light, the labyrinth of fern-laden shadows, weaved a tapestry of enchantment that lingered like an ancient hymn in the heart of the verdant wilderness.

A miraculous achievement. The complex labyrinth emerged within the maze of trees, a captivating world waiting to be explored. Lush gardens thrived, tended with cautious care, their grassy fields a victory for the community's tenacity. The wheat field swayed with a tranquil grace, bending to the whims of the gentle breeze. In the village's epicenter, a magnificent feast unfolded, with tables loaded with freshly harvested bounties from the land. The aroma of homemade dishes created a union that embraced all who gathered around.

The rover rumbled to a stop, and villagers, dressed in protective attire, congregated with expressions of both curiosity and hospitality. The driver stepped out of the vehicle and was met with genuine enthusiasm. Atlas and Charity followed suit, their gazes encompassing the community that encircled them. Charity ventured forward, her footsteps creating a soft crunch on the meticulously tended path beneath the dome as she entered. The surreal surroundings overwhelmed her senses, evoking an undeniable sense of wonder.

"They've built a life," she murmured, her astonishment turning the ordinary into the extraordinary. Atlas and Charity took off their respective masks and inhaled the pure, revitalizing oxygen the quarantine dome produced. For a moment, as they breathed in the crisp, clean air, they felt a profound sense of relief, to a world rejuvenated. They navigated the labyrinthine forest, each twist and turn potentially leading toward numerous paths. The maze of towering trees left Charity in awe; she couldn't resist reaching out to touch one, having only encountered them in books. The daughter began to grasp the significance of what trees meant in the old world, recognizing that they were not just majestic guardians of nature but life-givers that produced oxygen for humanity. Meanwhile, Atlas maintained his focus on the extraordinary civilization they were discovering within this verdant maze.

After exiting the forest, approaching with open hearts, the villagers welcomed Atlas and Charity as if they had discovered long-lost relatives. The fatigue from their journey made the invitation into this newfound tribe more compelling. They joined the villagers at the banquet table.

A sudden presence behind Charity jolted her nerves, and she spun around, her eyes wide with surprise. "No need to be alarmed, my dear. You must be starving after your journey. Eat with us," the driver reassured her, his voice a soothing tone.

The villagers worked in harmony, meticulously setting the table with a sense of care that mirrored their generosity. Despite the warm welcome, Atlas remained cautious, his concern for trust still apparent. A *woman* diligently swept the porch of a quaint shack. An *old man* sat in a rocking chair, immersed in his reading, while a *nun* delicately plucked potatoes from the garden. The banquet table was adorned with a pitcher of water and inviting dishes. Atlas and Charity took their seats, their oil-stained clothes contrasted sharply with the villagers' pristine attire.

The driver, his demeanor positive, moved with purpose, his intent clear in trying to ease their lingering unease. "Relax, you two. Enjoy, peace for a night," he spoke with genuine care.

Atlas continued observing the villagers with a watchful eye. This curious sight stirred a deep sense of discontent within him. Villagers moved about their daily tasks with an eerie synchronicity, engaged in a collective and ritualistic performance. Their actions were executed with precision, intensifying the mystery that cloaked this fascinating yet unsettling civilization. Atlas finally turned his attention to the driver, his voice tinged with anxiety. "What's with everyone wearing those masks?"

The driver responded with pride in his voice. "Symbolism."

Atlas persisted, seeking a more specific answer. "For what?"

The driver spoke candidly, his words carried meaning. "It's a reminder. Never take oxygen for granted."

The driver noticed Atlas's injured arm and carefully tended to it with hydrogen peroxide. A *muscular man* skillfully barbecued the grill, tending to sizzling meat with expertise. A *young girl* sitting across from Charity met her stare with playful curiosity, her eyes shining brightly beneath her bandit mask. The banquet table had a bountiful spread of vegetables and seasoned meats. Polite chatter filled the air as everyone eagerly anticipated the feast. The driver rose from his seat and gently tapped a glass with a spoon, causing all eyes to face Atlas and Charity. "To miracles. To Earth, the God of our civilization," he declared. "Let us pray for our planet to allow society another chance to start over."

Together, villagers participated in a collective meditation, their voices merging in a ritualistic chant. Charity sipped from her glass, while Atlas remained vigilant, his thoughts racing with inquiries. When the chant concluded, a festive mood swept over the gathering. Villagers indulged in the feast, savoring every bite and sip.

Beneath the visible cheer, there was trouble, a creeping shadow that spoke of impending danger drifting under the dome. Suddenly, the driver produced a *revolver*, pointing it directly at Atlas. The jovial ambiance froze, replaced by hostile glares from the villagers, their expressions shifting from joy to menace. The driver's voice cut through the tense silence, "It's not personal. It's about survival!"

Bang! The deafening gunshot pierced the air, shattering the fragile peace under the dome. In a swift move, Atlas dodged out of harm's way, narrowly avoiding the bullet that had been aimed at him. The bullet *ripped* and *tore* through the quarantine dome like knife on butter. Charity jolted almost out of her seat, the shock of the sudden violence surging through her like an electric current. From outside, the toxic gas infiltrated the dome, silently creeping inside. The villagers fell victim to its suffocating embrace one by one. An homage to the trials and tribulations of the haunting memory of the Holocaust. Panic erupted among the villagers as they scrambled for their alien masks.

Atlas and Charity, their eyes wide, swiftly secured their oxygen tanks. The father turned to his daughter and shouted, "Run!"

The driver, a dictator in his own right, commanded with ruthless authority over his tribe, evoking the memory of dictators like Hitler. "Kill them!" his order echoed with a chilling finality. With their alien masks, the villagers underwent a collective transformation, their actions coordinated with sinister synchronicity. Puppets pulled by an unseen puppeteer. The cheerful atmosphere of moments ago had dissolved into an unsettling unity of vindictive actions.

The daughter's instincts kicked in as she bolted away from the bloodthirsty scene. The rhythm of fear pounded in her ears, a desperate bid for escape from the enigmatic cult that had suddenly revealed its true nature. Charity scurried back into the forest, running through a complex network of tunnels. The dense evergreens surrounded her in a land that had once been God's country. Turning corner after corner, the daughter displayed undeniable resilience in her pursuit of escape. She pivoted her head and noticed alien villagers closing their distance, their alien-masked faces an odd sight.

During Charity's forest escape, madness erupted for Atlas. An alien villager lunged at him, driven by barbarism. In a swift, brutal response, Atlas's clenched fist connected solidly with the villager's jaw, sending a shockwave of pain through the attacker. The alien villager staggered backward, momentarily stunned by the unexpected blow. Atlas ran into the forest, his breath ragged. The bullets violently tore apart trees, narrowly missing his body.

Charity exited the forest and found herself in the twisted labyrinth of the small shacks within the village as her attackers continued to pursue. The narrow alleys seemed to close in on her, and at every turn, she never knew what was behind the corner. Fear and adrenaline coursed through her veins, urging her to run as fast as possible. Her legs burned from the exertion.

Her father was behind, his protective instincts drove him forward in an attempt to catch up. He glanced back, realizing that the alien villagers were a pack of wild hyenas, chasing him like a group of possessed animals. It was a maze of madness, where each turn and corner held the promise of uncertainty. The father and daughter were determined to break free from this surreal nightmare and find their way back to the road, where the environmental dangers of the world were at least familiar.

The daughter finally emerged from the quarantine dome, reentering the deadly world outside. Charity's eyes darted across an endless sea of sand and jagged rock formations. There was no shelter to be found in this terrestrial world. The quarantine dome loomed behind her, a cryptic reminder. A sanctuary turned prison, a place that promised safety but delivered only treacherous betrayal. Desperation set in as Charity realized the gargantuan size of the dystopian desert. The terrain was strangely familiar to Mars; instead of the red hue, a muted shade of brown was seen in all directions. With no clear path forward, she lifted her aqua eyes toward the flaming sky and hoped for a miracle. She looked for any kind of guidance in this bleak moment.

Atlas's face contorted in agony as the searing pain of a bullet struck his thigh. A surge of adrenaline coursed through his body as relentless violence surrounded him. An alien villager lunged at Atlas, both humans confronted each other with primal intensity. With savagery that harkened back to the earliest days of humanity, they grappled in the sand and fought for dominance. Their bodies carried the scars of countless battles. Each punch and strike were a reminder of the vicious struggle for survival in this alien realm. The alien villager fought with a wild determination. Atlas, his body battered and bloodied, countered with the hardened strength of a warrior who had faced the end of the world. They battled for supremacy, mirroring the ancient conflicts of early humanity, manifesting for dominance. It was an unspoken Cain and Abel narrative that played out, their rivalry etched a cautionary tale of human nature.

Atlas's battle with the alien villager served as a microcosm of the inhumanity that had gripped their reality. Despite the searing pain in his injured thigh, he called upon a surge of adrenaline-fueled toughness, every ounce of his remaining energy. In a display of raw power, he overpowered the alien villager, a visceral clash. The crack of gunfire rang out. Atlas executed an instantaneous maneuver, turning the alien villager around to use their body as a shield. Bullets ripped through the back of the alien villager, extinguishing their life in a hail of lead. Atlas discarded the lifeless body without hesitation and resumed his frantic sprint in the direction of his daughter.

In the backdrop of the hostile quarantine dome, Charity's anxious eyes fixated on a *graphite shed*, an out-of-place structure amidst the remoteness. She dashed toward it, her footsteps sending clouds of sand into the air. She ran faster, the wind whipping through her hair, as if her soul had taken flight. Desperation fueled her as she clutched the doorknob and pulled, but it remained stubbornly locked. She rammed her shoulder against the door. Luck eluded her as the door remained locked. The daughter stayed the course and continued bashing her shoulder against the door, the agony coursing through her with each impact. Despite her relentless efforts, she made no headway. The door was an impenetrable barrier, a insurmountable obstacle for her small frame.

Like a force of nature, Atlas charged toward her. His broad frame collided with the door, and it buckled under the combined fury of his effort. The powerful impact defeated the locked door, and with an ear-splitting creak, it gave way and swung open. Bullets struck the sturdy graphite structure. Atlas and Charity tumbled inside, finding a momentary asylum in the thick of their bedlam. The door slammed shut behind them, cutting off the insane world outside. Atlas knew they were trapped from all angles.

Inside the shed, stacks of graphite blocks, used for insulation against radiation, produced shadows in the flaming moonlight streaming through the skylight. The shattered door lent to their difficult situation as it refused to lock shut. Atlas grasped the handle with all the strength he could muster, using every vital force of his body as a roadblock. His shoulder dug into the door's frame, straining to hold it as securely as possible. Beside him, Charity stood resolute, her youthful energy assisted her father. Together, they lent their combined strength to the door's defense, a final effort against the horrors that lurked just beyond. Outside, the alien villagers launched a furious assault on the door as they slammed into it, their blows echoed like thunder. Atlas and Charity remained strong, refusing to budge an inch. Realizing the ineffectiveness of their efforts, the villagers changed tactics. They began to knock rhythmically on the walls of the shed, creating an unsettling sound. The knocking created a creepy noise; the villagers were playing a sinister game.

Atlas commanded his daughter, "Look for anything we can use as a weapon!"

Charity wandered further into the shed's darkness, her hands searching for any kind of weapon that could help. She found herself constantly moving in and out of the moonlight. Her foraging was derailed by a gruesome discovery. She stumbled into a *human body*, its skin peeled away, as it hung lifeless from the rafters. Shocked and horrified, she stumbled backward only to collide with another lifeless body, then another. The shed was filled with the haunting macabre of massacred corpses. Cannibalism, a practice shrouded in mystery, had indeed surfaced in the ancient world.

Now it had transformed into a modern phenomenon during the apocalypse, where starving humans would stop at nothing to obtain even a semblance of protein.

Outside, the pounding on the shed's walls by the savage villagers grew more intense. Their shouts and diabolical nature became increasingly distressing. *"We need to eat!"* Their cries reverberated, adding an unsettling layer to their horrendous cannibalism, tribal warfare screams.

Atlas, witnessing the horrifying scene and knowing what lay beyond the door, continued to use all his power to keep the door shut. Their lives were on death's doorstep. As the door creaked open, Atlas moved with lightning speed and slammed it shut once more. With every last-ditch ounce of his strength, he fought to seal out the cannibals. "Help me!" he cried out to his daughter, the urgency in his voice reflecting the problematic nature of their situation. Charity joined her father in bracing the door. Together, they stood against the primordial instincts of creatures, threatening to literally consume their lives. These were no longer humans, but obstructive physical specimens of hunger that demanded to be filled. Their primal instincts eclipsed the remains of their former humanity.

"We're going to die!"

"Not today!"

A *seismic rumbling* intensified. The ground beneath them vibrated violently as the shed shuddered under the immense force. A *sonic explosion* resonated through the air and the intense pounding from outside abruptly ceased. The menacing force that sought to break through the door retreated and was replaced by a solemn silence. It seemed that nature itself had intervened in their favor.

A faint pitter-patter of droplets fell on the roof. Atlas carefully swung open the door, his eyes scanning the transformed landscape. In a cataclysmic spectacle of nature's wrath, the earth convulsed, causing the dirt to explode upward. From the depths, a colossal column of *water* burst from underground, its majestic torrent cascaded like a divine revelation.

Atlas and Charity scrambled from the graphite shed. The alien villagers, captivated and stunned by the water's ferocity, converged around the erupting *geyser*. The water gushed forth with powerful force. Alien villagers darted and weaved, narrowly avoiding the tumbling rocks that accompanied the flood of water.

With a swift and brutal swing, Atlas bashed one of the alien villagers with his shovel as a makeshift weapon. He searched the fallen adversary and retrieved a *pistol*, then slung the shovel back over his shoulder with the secured rope. Atlas took aim at the approaching alien villagers, his finger steady on the trigger. Shots rang out, each one finding its intended target with impressive accuracy. "Follow me!" The father and daughter moved in tandem, their path filled with danger but driven by the instinct to escape the belligerent environment.

The father and daughter dashed toward the waiting planetary rover as the formidable geyser continued to produce water. The alien villagers kneeled in reverence before the unstoppable event, their hands outstretched in prayer to the Earth. They paid tribute to the God of water.

Charity scrambled into the back of the rover and felt the torrential downpour drench her as she sought safety.

The driver, driven by his obsessive pursuit, tackled Atlas from behind, their bodies colliding heavily onto the platform. Atlas, grappling with pain, fought to break free, his injured leg a hefty burden. The driver preached, "This is our awakening! Stay with us!"

Water continued to pour down like a flood cleansing everything it desired to touch. The fight between Atlas and the driver escalated as they wrestled each other onto the surface of the rover's platform. Each move, each clash, was a battle for control in a high-stakes contest of strength and will. The cannibalistic tribe, their hunger dissatisfied, raced relentlessly toward the rover.

Atlas turned his attention toward Charity, his eyes locked onto the approaching cannibals. "Drive!" The rover's engine sprung to life as the vehicle lurched forward, carrying the father, daughter, and driver away from the starving alien villagers.

Inside the rover, Charity floored the accelerator, propelling the vehicle forward with increasing speed. Outside on the platform, Atlas gripped the shovel with all his might, then swung it, hitting the driver square in the face. The force of the blow sent the driver backward before he plunged off the platform. He grabbed the edge and hung on for dear life while the rover dragged his body across the desert. A melee of alien villagers attempted to board the rover, but Atlas continued his impressive assault. Blow after blow, he fended off their advances with the shovel, the powerful strikes knocked them back and prevented them from getting on board. With each swing, Atlas defended their only means of escape. The alien villagers, overwhelmed by his fierce strength, found themselves repelled one by one. The rover, its tires churning through the muddy terrain, accelerated away from the desperate tribe, leaving the disorientated villagers in its muddy wake.

Atlas took a moment to catch his breath, his chest heaving with exhaustion. He turned his attention back to Charity. Behind him, the driver, despite his injuries, managed to pull himself back up onto the platform. He raised his revolver and aimed it at Atlas. *Bang! Bang!* Two shots rang out. A searing pain shot through Atlas's side as an armor-piercing bullet punctured his oblique. Despite the agony, Atlas summoned his strength and fired a shot between the driver's eyes, ending his life. His lifeless body tumbled off the platform like a rag doll as it crashed onto the sand, marking the conclusion of their tumultuous confrontation.

Atlas dropped to his knees, his breath coming and going. The man felt every inch of the last bullet; the pain penetrated deep inside his battered body. He grimaced and watched as the water geyser continued its destructive path, tearing through the quarantine dome, dismantling it piece by piece. With blood running down his trembling hand, Atlas reached for a button on the control panel and pressed it, causing the platform to close, sealing off the rover from the outside. The rover drove through the cascading water geyser, gradually clearing the area.

Inside the rover, Charity's concern grew as she noticed the gunshot wound on her father's side. "Dad, we have to stop!" she begged, her voice harnessed with worry. Atlas remained focused. He refused to succumb to his injury. "You're bleeding really bad!" Charity said, her voice filled with concern.

"Get back on the main road," Atlas pointed ahead, his determination unwavering despite the pain that gnawed at him.

The rover traversed the bleak badlands as they drove by majestic mountains that had crumbled into towering heaps of ash. The sky above was cloaked in an eerie green hue, a reminder of the venomous toxic gases that had poisoned the atmosphere. Gray ash descended from the sky as though they were in an eternal limbo, symbolic of Earth's tragic transformation.

Exhaustion and pain began to wear down Atlas. He felt his strength waning as his eyes grew heavy.

"Dad, wake up!" Charity pleaded, her aqua eyes divided between the road and her ailing father. Atlas lost consciousness, slumping in his seat. Charity, left to her own devices, faced the daunting task of finding the coast on her own; her subconscious knew their journey was far from over.

*   *   *

Within the realm of dreams, Atlas found himself in an endless tunnel of bones, submerged by countless skeletons. A wormhole of the dead. The skeletons emitted hazy fumes that filled the confined space with mist and fog. A gravelly, resonant voice emanated from the shadows. "Mother Nature is both creator and destroyer…"

Atlas's words echoed through the void of bones. The man stretched out his hands, his fingers grasping through the atmosphere as he searched for answers. An ear-splitting *roar* intensified and grew louder, moving closer with each passing moment. A *rush of water* hurtled toward Atlas, an unstoppable force of nature. It engulfed him and pulled him into the darkness.

*   *   *

The rover came to a halt in a *coastal town* where the arrow of time had etched its story into the soul of the place. Here, the forgotten sea carried memories of time's lost tides. Ash flakes descended from the fiery sky. Fragments of wooden buildings barely remained, their aged structures mimicked pages of an ancient book. It was a coastal town that had long since slipped away. In the days of old, humans regarded these places as the most magical wonders on Earth.

The pure poetry of the ocean had been swallowed by the depths of hell. Its serene verses were silenced, leaving behind a world where the soothing music of waves had turned into a mournful elegy. Rumors, like murmurs of ancient secrets, caressed the wind, suggesting that water may exist beneath the hidden chambers of the world. Although the odds of such a discovery were slim, it remained the best place to search for water. It was a palpable marvel how this coastal town, against the odds, still had fragments of its structures despite the Earth's apocalypse. In the distance, the majestic lighthouse stood. Its light, once a guiding star for sailors on stormy nights, now stood extinguished.

Within this forgotten place, Charity and her unconscious father found themselves at a crossroads. The coast, throughout human history, had carried the enchantment of wishes. This place, a former dream-weaver, had long ago surrendered the art of granting wishes. The genie in the bottle was forever encased in the sands of limbo as it whispered wishes into the patient ears of eternity, waiting for a release that may never come.

Inside the rover while the first light of dawn filtered through the windows, Charity's voice cut through the air. She shook her father who lay unresponsive. "Dad, wake up!"

Atlas was silent. The father remained lost in the depths of unconsciousness where the struggle for survival never slept.

Charity stepped out of the rover and entered the eerie quietness of the coastal town. She scanned the area, her eyes searching for any sign of life in this forsaken place. "Somebody help me!" the daughter screamed at the top of her lungs.

Desperation fueled her movements until she spotted a distant *flashing light* at the top of the lighthouse. Without hesitation, she sprinted toward it, her feet pounding the drylands. Charity waved her arms frantically, her gestures a plea for assistance, a cry for help. "My dad's injured!"

She pushed the door open and entered the lighthouse. Charity's steps echoed in the broad space, her senses overwhelmed by the juxtaposition of its resilient castle architecture. The monolithic walls and worn brick flooring spoke of an ancient monument withstanding the apocalypse.

The daughter aimed the pistol as she approached the rusted iron spiral staircase. The stairs twisted, leading her upwards towards an uncertain destination. Each step was obscured by a layer of dark soot, veiling any trace of previous occupants. "Is anybody alive?" Charity's voice rang through the hollow structure, followed by echoes. Nobody responded to her poignant call of the searching soul. The stairs seemed endless as they wound and turned in a mesmerizing pattern. Eventually, Charity reached a door and, without hesitation, pushed it open, her heart pounding in anticipation. The creaking door unfurled a room bathed in the glowing inferno of sunlight. An arched window overlooked the nightmare coast, its frame encrusted with salt and grime.

Inside the lighthouse's tower, Charity's eyes darted around, taking in the debris-strewn room. Old newspaper articles littered the floor, their headlines detailed the planet's devastating drought. A torn Genesis Bible, its pages ripped, lay abandoned. Anthropology and science books, their spines cracked and well-worn, were scattered. With a curious touch, Charity gathered some of the newspaper articles and tattered biblical pages, reading the tales of humanity's downfall. The walls were a surreal portrait of Darwinian evolution diagrams, mingled with religious verses from the Holy Vedas and Tibetan Book of the Dead. They blurred the lines between science and faith.

Against the wall, a laboratory stood as a vestige to the bygone pursuit of knowledge. Medical equipment, instruments, and disheveled papers were on the wooden floor. In the center of the room rested an ancient *skeleton*. Near the skeleton stood an oak desk adorned with a vintage typewriter and microscope. On the wall hung the evocative painting by Hieronymus Bosch, 'Garden of Earthly Delights', a reflection of human desires and the complexity of existence. Charity's attention was captured by a motionless robot seated at the desk. Its rusted metal frame had decayed from the viciousness of time. Even robots couldn't survive the apocalypse. Their metal bodies and electromagnetic minds succumbed to the new laws of nature on Earth.

The broken world seemed to conspire against Charity. As she neared the motionless robot, her world was upended with a deafening *crack!* Beneath her feet, the floorboard gave way, and she plummeted through the crumbling wood. A frantic gasp escaped her lips as she spiraled downward. The pistol she carried desperately slipped from her grasp, clattering against the weathered floor.

With a *jolt* of unexpected movement, the robot came to life. Its rusty joints groaned and creaked as it awakened from its dormant state. Its mechanical fingers handily reached for the fallen pistol on the floor. The room, filled with tension, became a chess match between the human and robot. Charity had read about such enigmas built long ago that were supposed to lighten the load for humanity, which they did in their programmed way. The last war on Earth wasn't fought against robots and artificial intelligence. During the end of the days, robots were technological protectors that stood by humanity's side until the very end.

The room was filled with uncertainty as the robot had possession of the pistol. Its glowing eyes fixated on Charity, the human intruder who now faced a sentient machine. The robot was neither ally nor enemy, but a sentinel of a world long gone wrong. The robot's mechanical voice emerged, "Are you trying to rob me, little girl?"

The daughter remained defiant, "No! I need help!"

The robot was stoic and mockingly responded, "That's what they all say. I can't trust anyone anymore."

Charity remained confident within herself, "I'm a good person."

The robot's laughter echoed against the walls, "Spare me your empty promises. The concept of good has been destroyed by evil."

On her knees, Charity pleaded to the robot, "Please, my father needs help. Do you have any water?"

The robot unimpressed by her plea remained logical in its response, "Water, the elixir of life, how precious it once was."

Charity's stare remained focused, her aqua eyes locked onto the robot's glowing optical sensors. She was not afraid of the machine. An intense stand-off, their intentions clashed in the otherworldly atmosphere. "I need water, and I need it now!"

"That's your problem."

"He's going to die!"

An abrupt gunshot from the pistol aimed at the brick ceiling disrupted the tension in the room. The bullet deflected off the fortress of thick brick. The robot's mechanical demeanor underwent a sudden transformation. "Get up now!" the machine wallowed.

Charity slowly stood to her feet, her eyes never leaving the mysterious robot. It was impossible to read any emotions. The confrontation remained suspended in a taut stillness. Charity was uncertain of the next turn in this strange encounter.

The robot pointed to the wall, "See that painting?"

Charity remained unresponsive, refusing to listen to the order given by the robot. Another gunshot pierced the ceiling, causing Charity to flinch. She pivoted toward the artwork of Hieronymus Bosch's 'Garden of Earthly Delights' that demanded her attention. She was captivated by the canvas, which teemed with fantastical creatures and bizarre, transcendental landscapes. The painting was made up of three palettes, each one told a specific story about humanity's evolution.

"Homo sapiens had their chance to thrive, yet they let the dance of destruction choreograph their journey. Now, the flood of extinction condemns all. Your kind were blind witnesses to the planet's cries, warned of the impending reckoning. Ignorance isn't bliss; it's the veil behind which guilt finds comfort. Retribution is a consequence written in the archives of time," the robot lectured.

Charity defended herself, "I'm not like them." She was irresistibly drawn to the puzzling painting; its cryptic web of riddles engaged her attention.

The first palette of the painting offered a vivid visual representation of the Genesis story, illustrating themes of creation, temptation, and the ramifications of human actions. The second palette delved into the concept of purgatory through its depictions of sin, suffering, and the potential for redemption. The chaotic imagery hinted at the idea that humanity's earthly actions may lead to a state of doom. The third palette portrayed an inferno of divine punishment. The nightmarish scenes illustrated the culmination of sin and descent into hell, highlighting the eternal conclusion of the apocalyptic aftermath.

The robot's mechanical eyes remained focused on the painting as if to search for answers within the specific details of the imagery. "Genesis represented the act of creation, a moment when possibilities flourished. Until humanity left that sacred path and descended into a state of limbo, neglecting their duty to protect the Earth. Now, we find ourselves in the heart of an inferno, where the world is swallowed by the jaws of the apocalypse."

Charity stood her ground, defending herself. "I want to save our world."

The robot changed the subject, reminiscing about its past life. "I was a professor once."

"Nice to meet you. I'm…"

"I didn't ask what your name is!"

"I'm not afraid of you."

"Good. I'm nothing… Just a robot… Go to the window, human."

"Please…"

"Go to the window or I'll kill you."

"Let me say goodbye to my father. He's all I have left."

"I don't care."

Charity wandered forward. Her footsteps echoed in the silence of the room as she approached the window, her movements deliberate with uncertainty. Her aqua eyes scanned the scenery that unfolded before her. The world outside, a funereal gray, overpowered the sun's brilliance and created a shroud over the Earth.

The robot stared into her soul. "Don't turn around…"

Charity underwent a hypnotic trance while staring at the waterless ocean. She was met with a haunting view, an abyss of emptiness that stretched out into infinity. This was the world's reality, a void of desolation where mighty waves once roared, now reduced to lifeless rocks of parched seabeds. The ocean was eerily comparable to the singularity of a black hole. Darkness was everywhere, the consequences of humanity's foolishness. The silence of this underwater wasteland enveloped her. The magical oceanic depths, a past realm of wonder and mystery, have been stripped of their vitality. Charity contemplated the depths of this bottomless pit—a reflection of the world above and the profound loss it represented. The planet, forever altered, spoke a truth to the daughter, immersing her in its transfiguration.

"What do you see?"

"Nothing."

The robot pontificated philosophically, "The dark is what you see when you go to sleep for the last time. Darwin was right. Chance made humanity. Not the divine creator. Free will destroyed everything."

Charity closed her aqua eyes, "Make it fast."

The robot raised the pistol, "Are you ready for the unknown?"

The impact of the world's devastation submerged her. Charity braced herself and waited for the next move as the robot held her hostage. It was a world where the familiar has become alien, where rationality was a distant memory.

"Just let me say goodbye…"

"Remember me when you tell this story…"

In that moment where time itself seemed to stop, the robot put the pistol inside its own metallic mouth and pulled the trigger, terminating itself. Metal fragments scattered across the room, leaving Charity alone. The daughter's eyelids slowly parted; she was grateful to find herself alive.

She rushed to the desk, frantically rummaging through its drawers. She discovered a bottle of water. Relief washed over her as she clutched the rare natural resource, her only hope for her ailing father.

Charity's adrenaline rushed as she sprinted toward the rover. Her father's life hung in the balance, and she knew she had to protect him at all costs. In the distance, she spotted two spirit gas mask *vagrants*, their cruel intentions clear as they attempted to rob her father of his oxygen tank.

The gas masks were a grotesque fusion of Hindu and Buddhist symbolism and emanated an aura of evil spirituality. Amidst humanity's descent, even deities like Shiva and Buddha would weep in bitter remorse for the cataclysm their creations had birthed. Survival was the ultimate prize that demanded vigilance, for any moment of weakness invited the predation of the strong upon the vulnerable.

Charity raised the pistol and fired two shots into the sky. The sound cut through the quietness. Danger lurked around every corner and nowhere on Earth was safe. The spirit gas mask vagrants froze in their tracks, their hands raised in surrender. The shots served as a warning, a declaration that Charity would not be intimidated or defeated. The vagrants backed away and sprinted from the rover. Charity's confidence remained unshaken for her father's sake.

Inside the rover, Charity acted swiftly, sealing the unit shut to keep the dangerous air at bay. She kneeled beside her father, her eyes filled with concern. Gently, she lifted Atlas's head and brought the water bottle to his cracked lips. With a careful tilt, she urged him to drink, the water trickling down his dry throat. "Drink, Dad. Please."

Atlas obeyed, taking small sips of the precious liquid, his strength slowly returning. He pushed the bottle away, signaling that he had enough. "I remember when I used to do that for you…" A tender smile graced both of their faces. It was a moment of warmth in the darkness that surrounded them. The father passed the water bottle back to his daughter. "You finish it…"

Charity hesitated for a moment, casting a concerned look toward her father before she ultimately complied. She finished the last drops of water, knowing every valuable molecule must be consumed.

"Let me see the gun," Atlas said. The daughter handed the pistol to her father, who inspected it methodically, his experienced hands examining the weapon's condition.

"One more left."

"Sorry. I thought those people were going to kill you."

"Don't apologize. You did good." Atlas looked at his daughter. He couldn't help but feel a profound sense of pride in her resilience. She had come a long way. He understood the difficult choices they had to make along their journey. Having reached the coast and unearthed their new home in the form of the lighthouse, their quest demanded a profound pursuit of another hidden treasure: The underground water source, the pulse of their newfound oasis. Atlas rallied his remaining strength and stood tall. The fire in his soul still burned brightly as he urged his daughter forward, ready to begin the task of digging for their chance at a second life. "Let's start digging…"

Together, the father and daughter wandered toward the coastline. The void, which used to be the ocean, was a reminder of the test they had faced and the challenges that lie ahead. Only the familiar ancient sands of time on the beach were familiar. On the coast, where the waterless ocean met the land, the horizon shimmered like a mirage, a surreal dreamscape of endless rocks that seemed to stretch into eternity. The rocks were prehistoric relics, jagged forms rising from the drought-stricken seabed. These rocks were prehistoric elements that built the planet from nothing, guarding secrets buried beneath the salt-encrusted surface. The man's mind wandered back in time to when dinosaurs roamed those same shores, marveling at how much had changed in the eons since their existence.

Atlas drove the shovel into the limitless sand. Each brutal strike produced shockwaves of pain through his aching limbs. His body had undergone an insurmountable amount of punishment. Beside him, Charity stood guard, clutching the pistol. After digging for some time, Atlas, a former pillar of strength, leaned heavily on the shovel. Every labored breath was a tribute to the unforgiving trials of survival that penetrated his body and mind, carrying a magnitude of scars with countless battles he waged against the apocalypse.

"Maybe I should try, Dad?"

"Good idea."

With a nod, he relinquished the shovel to his daughter. Charity took hold of the worn handle, their eyes locked in a voiceless understanding that she would carry the torch of survival. Atlas eased himself onto the gritty sand, his strength depleted. The man had exhausted his energy reserves; everything was harder than before, his physicality had aged significantly during their adventurous journey to the coast. "Take your time," he rasped. "We've got a long way to go."

Charity dug with uncompromising purpose; her every haul of the shovel revealed the profound resilience she had developed over their odyssey. Atlas's eyes shifted from the lighthouse to his daughter; the girl he once knew evolved into a formidable woman. Every father's dream was to watch their little girl grow up; he found peace in this moment. Charity dug deeper into the sand, her desperation was matched only by her tenacity. With each shovelful of earth cast aside, she grappled with the inefficacy of her efforts, the hidden water remained stubbornly elusive underground. This endeavor would take some time.

She continued to dig until, from the ether, a *surge* of *gravitational pressure* gripped the world, unleashing an intense energy that seemed to emerge from the core of Earth. A sudden, forceful pain shot through Charity's chest, robbing her of breath and sending her tumbling to the gritty sand. The shovel slipped from her grasp, clattering to the ground. Atlas felt a similar discomfort gnawed at his own chest and pivoted toward the lighthouse.

Unseen forces wreaked havoc upon the structure, causing it to *splinter* and *crack*. The gravitational forces that had once held everything firmly in place *inverted* and *crushed* all within it inward. Atlas summoned a reserve of strength he didn't know he had. He seized the shovel and drove it into the sand with a frenzied urgency. His muscles strained against the unnatural resistance, every muscle aching. With each grueling shovel of sand, the father engaged in a battle to defy the force of gravity. The force that had created all was now destroying everything in its path. The father dug deeper and created an improvised underground shelter where he pulled Charity into the hole, shielding her from the escalating gravitational onslaught above ground. Atlas positioned himself over Charity as a human shield, his body braced against the crushing force, determined to protect his daughter.

Above ground, the surface *quivered* and *contorted* under the inverted gravitational phenomena. The father could feel the phantasmagorical pull, a wild and untamed energy that held mysteries beyond human comprehension.

The Earth's core rumbled, and with a deafening roar, the lighthouse surrendered to the overwhelming force. Piece by piece, its ancient architecture crumbled into an uproar vortex of debris that hurtled *upward* into the sky.

Suddenly, Atlas and Charity were *yanked* into the sky. Chaos theory had ascended to a profound new level of understanding. They found themselves suspended in a state of weightlessness, adrift in the sky. Higher and higher they rose, their ascent ever escalating into rarefied realms like intrepid explorers scaling the dizzying peaks of possibility. Abruptly, gravity relinquished its hold, and Atlas, Charity, and the shattered remnants of the lighthouse plummeted back to the ground. The trio crashed onto the sand; their prospective home was destroyed by the anomaly's cruel touch.

Atlas and Charity lay sprawled on the sand, their bodies battered and bruised by the violent impact. The strange, otherworldly physics event had run its course, leaving them injured but miraculously alive. The daughter crawled over to join her father. They rested together on the coast, sharing the panoramic view of the waterless ocean. A serene silence draped over them, as though the world dared not disturb the tranquility of the supernatural environment. The depth of the ocean was an eternal pit, an immeasurable crater that consumed the planet.

From the depths of Earth, powerful eruptions emerged. Underneath the barren seabed, *volcanoes* roared to life, discharging *molten* fury. Lava, a magical element, surged forth from its subterranean prison. One of the mass extinction events of Earth's history, when volcanoes erupted worldwide, left a haunting parallel to the current cataclysmic event that was unfolding. Fiery plumes surged skyward, engulfing the world in an ominous cloud of darkness.

The air thickened with black soot and ash, releasing a cloak upon the planet. It was as if the Grim Reaper, wielding a scythe, had descended upon them. This catastrophic upheaval triggered a *dimming effect*, plunging everything into darkness. It was a doppelgänger event comparable to the Triassic-Jurassic extinction event, where dinosaurs met the same fate.

"Do you think we deserved this?"

"Our planet had no choice… Maybe one day, we'll learn to listen to Earth."

"I wish I could have seen the ocean."

Atlas's weary eyes locked onto the decaying, weathered pier further down the forsaken coast. He summoned the last remains of his strength and while using the shovel as his makeshift crutch, slowly rose from the sand.

"I want to show you something."

"You should rest."

Atlas stretched out his bloodied, gloved hand toward Charity, a wordless assurance. "I can rest later," the father whispered. With his gentle help, Atlas lifted Charity to her feet, and together, they embarked on another leg of their seemingly endless journey. The father released his grip on the shovel, allowing it to rest on the coast.

Atlas and Charity walked in silence along the deserted boardwalk. The grimy *Ferris wheel* cast a shadow upon them, its rusted structure holding on for dear life. A roller coaster track weaved through the decaying framework. Charity's eyes wandered to the game stands, their prizes forgotten and covered in dust. Rows of faded, stuffed animals stared with vacant eyes, an evocative vestige of the humans who once found joy here.

"What are we doing, Dad?"

"We're walking."

"What about the lighthouse?"

"I have a plan…"

Atlas harbored a secret, a revelation of sorts. All he wanted now was to cherish their time together. In this part of the world, there remained a peculiar difference. Earth, while not fully revived, held onto a hint of life, as if the coast retained a fragment of enlightenment.

Atlas reflected, "After your mom told me she was pregnant with you, we just walked around here. Time froze. We forgot about the future of our world... Until time, like a dream, drifted away, leaving us with only faded memories." Atlas placed his arm around his daughter's shoulder, gently relaxing her. This important moment was precious for the weak man.

* * *

Atlas and Angelica wore their protective suits and swayed together beneath the crimson glow of the moon. Above, the sky cried ashes from the erupting volcanoes. The flakes of death sprinkled over the husband and wife. They shared a slow dance, their figures illuminated by the inferno light, a hauntingly beautiful moment amidst the backdrop of an apocalyptic Earth.

* * *

Hand in hand, Atlas and Charity set forth on a peaceful stroll along the pier's edge, a rare backdrop of tranquility within the tempestuous tides of their globe-trotting experience. These memories, however fleeting, were the threads of life, weaving a poignant reminder of the enduring love that bound a father and daughter and transcended the trials of their world.

"We always talked about bringing you here after you were born.

"Why didn't you?"

"Mom died... along with Earth..."

Atlas extended his hand and captured a drifting speck of gray ash in his glove, a symbol of how Earth had irrevocably altered the course of humanity. It was a lesson not to overlook the true God that was inherent in the fabric of reality. Atlas and Charity, humble earthly disciples, observed Mother Nature and awaited her revelation of intentions, whatever they might be, with reverence for the timeless wisdom she held. These facets of life, profound in their lessons, should be preserved within a time capsule, a timeless treasure for all future generations of humanity to observe and cherish down the winding road of history.

The father and daughter sat in a dilapidated Ferris wheel cart, its decaying frame creaked while it rocked gently back and forth in the dying light. Their masks reflected the inferno sunlight as it entered its slumber, allowing the emergence of twilight. On the horizon, foreboding shadows came into being, a harbinger of the approaching dark gray clouds.

Beneath the shimmering crescent moon, the North Star illuminated from the vacuum of space. The father came to a halt, his weary steps ceased as the realization settled upon him. They had nowhere else to go, no path left untraveled. The man was keenly aware that their dystopian reality was inescapable. There were no more secret plans. Indeed, there was no grand escape plan or secret strategy, only a profound life lesson he wished to pass on: Don't ever give up, no matter the odds. This was the enduring philosophical mantra that he shared with his daughter that would guide her through the darkest of times.

Charity's mind moved silently, her innermost self reached out in a wordless plea, a prayer for the miraculous to unfold.

The father turned to his daughter. "May I have this dance?" Charity, quite taken aback, blushed as any daughter would in such a situation.

"Dad?"

Atlas chuckled softly, a hint of irony in his voice. "Just in case you don't ever get married," he teased. "I want to at least dance with my daughter once in my life." A moonlight glow submerged the world. Atlas gently extended his hand, inviting Charity to join him in a slow dance. Charity accepted his proposal. They swayed gently; their forms silhouetted against the lunar glow. Charity rested her head upon her father's chest, the rhythmic thumping of his heart a reassuring lullaby. Time stood still and the world became, if only briefly, a perfect place.

Emerging from the twilight, the first rumbles of *thunder* and flickers of *lightning* painted the distant horizon. The initial drops of *rain* descended a delicate murmur upon parched Earth. Gradually, it crescendoed into a zealous downpour. Each drop's collision with the ground was a miraculous symphony, as the harmonious whispers of life echoed throughout the coast.

The father and daughter raised their masked faces to the heavens, their forms stoic during the watery avalanche. The father looked towards the heavens, "So that's what it feels like."

The daughter mirrored her father's actions. "We're going to make it!"

The tranquil scene was ruptured by an insistent, mechanical *beep... beep... beep!* The alarm resounded through the air, a harsh reminder of their fragile existence. The beeping grew more frantic, each beep a cruel tick of the clock.

It held a dire truth: Atlas's oxygen supply was depleted. As he struggled for breath, he slowly eased himself to the pier. The father, weathered by time, embraced death's shadow with stoic acceptance. He was ready to dance with Father Time. The daughter wasn't prepared to bid farewell, but in the wisdom of her soul, she knew that death, an inevitable visitor, ultimately arrived to claim all.

Charity, her eyes wide with concern, joined her father on the ground. With trembling hands, Atlas fumbled for the straps of his welder mask. He unfastened it, revealing his world-weary face etched with scars of life. The tainted air greedily infiltrated his lungs; the father continued his battle until his final breath. Atlas's raspy voice cut through the sound of the rain, holding dearly onto its fading strength. "You wear it now."

Raindrops mixed with tears as Charity cradled her father in her arms, their bodies drenched by the cleansing downpour. In unison, they gazed towards the heavens, their souls intertwined as they shared a moment of profound serenity, a divine communion in the middle of the unfolding miracle.

With trembling fingers, Atlas retrieved the compass necklace from his pocket. He stared at it for a lingering moment before extending it toward Charity. "Do me a favor. Keep this close."

"Please, don't leave me. I'll never see you again."

The father held his daughter close, aware of life exiting his soul, the ebbing of vitality as he grappled with his ending. "My brave girl, you'll always carry a part of me in your heart. Let your heart be your compass. I'm proud of the woman you've become. Thank you for being born. Remember, never lose… hope…"

Atlas's voice faded as his eyes gently closed for the final time. Charity's head nestled against her father's chest as the tears flowed freely. The pistol rested nearby, holding a single bullet in its chamber, a silent witness to the heartfelt goodbye.

Raindrops pelted the welder mask, each drop a priceless gift from nature, that allowed life to emerge again from the ashes. It was a rebirth from reality, a transcendental awakening that unfolded like an ancient scroll of enlightenment. Just like the first molecules materialized from the vacuum of space, an embryonic genesis ushered in the symphony of life.

The daughter, drawing upon the depths of her psyche, found the fortitude to speak in her subconscious. "After years had passed, the rain returned. Its arrival breathed life into our brown world, as blue was reborn. Water once again graced our Earth, offering us a second chance." Charity stood to her feet, her eyes glistening with tears of gratitude as she watched the water replenish the planet.

She reached for the welder mask and held it delicately in her hands. Charity placed the welder mask on her face, a lasting keepsake of her father that carried his invincible spirit forward into this new world. The daughter stood at the edge of the pier and gazed out upon the ocean, embracing the extraordinary resurrection unfolding before her. "My wish for humanity is to strive for improvement in our next endeavor, to nurture the flame of hope, and promise a future for the next generation on Earth."

The rain intensified and poured down with increasing passion, filling the air with anticipation. In the sky, a new beginning arrived. Another opportunity dawned for humanity, allowing in uncharted waters of the future, guided by the wisdom of the past. The rain fell harder. From the clouds, a *rainbow* emerged, painting the magical spectrum across the Earth.

The End

WATER IS OUR CREATOR.
NEVER TAKE IT FOR GRANTED.

PARABLE

If God is for us, who can be against us?
Bible

Land of Eternity

In a world far beyond our reach existed a curious realm known as the Land of Eternity. In this land, a parable unfolded, a tale of immortality, that echoed the myths of Sisyphus and the allegory of Plato's cave. In the Land of Eternity, its inhabitants were granted the gift of everlasting life. They reveled in their newfound immortality, achieving feats that mortals could only dream of. They amassed riches, garnered fame, and reached the pinnacle of human accomplishment. Pulitzer Prizes, Nobel Prizes, billionaire status, celebrity acclaim—they conquered it all. As their existence stretched into infinity, they began to sense a shadow on the horizon, a lingering question that no success could overcome. They turned their conscious minds to the universe, pondering the fate of their eternal home. For even in their immortal state, they realized a bitter truth.

The sun above them was their eternal companion. But it, too, had an appointment with destiny, an explosive finale, a supernova that would consume their beloved Earth. As they grappled with this cosmic inevitability, another truth dawned upon them. Even if they were to somehow outlive the sun's fiery demise, they could not escape the cold, dark grasp of the universe's heat death, a fate sealed by the anomaly of entropy.

In their existential quandary, they contemplated the paradox of the universe, a cyclical, divergent vacuum that perpetually birthed matter. Could it be that, in the grand majestical nature of existence, they were destined to repeat their journey? That within an eternal amount of time, everything might be recycled once more?

The Land of Eternity was filled with philosophers, scientists, and dreamers who pondered these questions, much like Sisyphus who pushed his boulder and Plato's prisoners in the cave, controlled by their illusions. They came to understand that, regardless of their immortality, there were forces beyond their control, forces that shaped the destiny of worlds and galaxies. And so, the tale of immortality taught them a profound lesson. It whispered that, even in the face of eternity, there were mysteries that would forever elude their grasp. It urged them to embrace the beauty of the moment, to cherish their fading experiences and to seek connection with their species.

For in the end, whether mortal or immortal, humanity's quest for understanding would persist, a spark of curiosity that flickered throughout the cycles of time, forever seeking to illuminate the darkness of the unknown.

Stephon Stewart
Author. Theorist. Filmmaker.

Stewart crafts metaphysical stories and fantasy thrillers infused with Nostradamus themes. In his inaugural narrative film, "PSYCHE," he embarked on an odyssey through the labyrinthine corridors of the human mind, a quest to unearth the meaning of life. With artificial intelligence as the antagonist and protagonist, the film navigates the complexities of consciousness in a cinematic exploration that promises to be both enlightening and thought-provoking. Stewart's deep concern for humanity's future has been a driving force behind his work, notably his creation "DRY." The dystopian story was also adapted into a compelling graphic novel. The book and graphic novel serve as a testament to Stewart's dedication to ignite hope and drive action for the transformation toward a sustainable solution for future generations.

Beyond his creative pursuits, Stewart's artistic vision extends to the canvas, where he paints depictions of potential Earth scenarios if we neglect our planet. This surreal artwork, now featured on climate-conscious apparel under the name "GLOBAL TRANSFIGURATION" reflects his passion for environmental ethics.

Amidst his artistic and writing endeavors, Stewart continues to delve into physics, further enriching his knowledge of the universe and reality. His collaboration with a neuroscientist has led to a groundbreaking theory published in the Open Journal for Biophysics. This innovative work focuses on unblocking blood vessels and addressing clogged arteries with an aim to extend life. His scientific contributions are available for exploration on Google Scholar.

Stewart's multifaceted journey threads storytelling, art, science, and a commitment to unveil the logical truth of reality to humanity. Through this blend of disciplines, he seeks to illuminate the mysteries of existence, by inspiring contemplation in the hearts and minds of those who encounter his work.